Lethal Flip

A Home Renovator Mystery

by

M. E. Bakos

This book is fiction. All characters, events, and organizations portrayed in this novel are the product of the author's imagination or are used fictitiously. Any resemblance to actual persons—living or dead—is entirely coincidental. The home improvement tips given in LETHAL FLIP are not to be used in lieu of professional help. Author does not make any warranties about the completeness, reliability and accuracy of this information. Any use of home improvement tips is at reader's risk.

For information: email mebakos@yahoo.com

Ingram Print: ISBN 979-8-9850770-8-7
Amazon Print: ISBN 979-8-9850770-2-5
B&N Print: ISBN 979-8-9850770-5-6

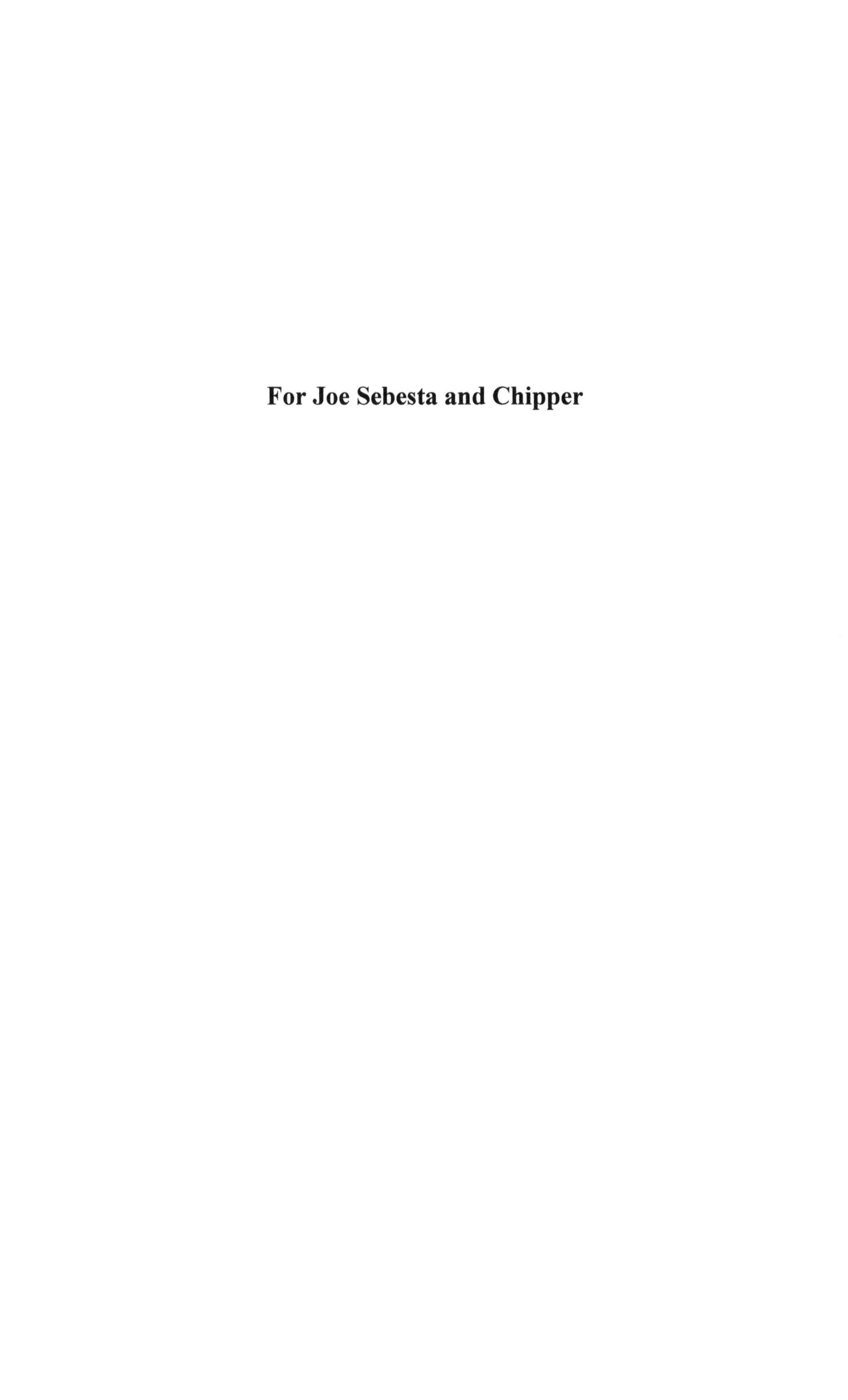

For Joe Sebesta and Chipper

PROLOGUE

We met the ghostbuster in Hiptown in the sleepy, early dawn at the site where my last flip had gone terribly wrong. My name is Katelyn Baxter and I'm a Home Rehab Specialist. Renewing houses is my passion.

"I'm Bernie. Glad to meet you!" He stuck out his hand and gripped my BFF Myra Alexandria Payten's hand. He turned to me and did the same, saying, "I specialize in moving spirits into the light, perform weddings, and I'm a Lyft driver. When you call me, you get a full-service ghostbuster, driver, and wedding official!" He delivered his spiel in a high-pitched voice, grinning, showing coffee-stained teeth. He appeared to be a slick operator with dark eyes and brown wiry hair which was thinning on top. His trim build was solid. I guessed him to be thirtysomething.

The wild look in his eye matched the intensity of his energy. He toted a boom box and a backpack. He unzipped his pack to display several sage bundles. He focused his piercing look on Myra. "We're going to get this ghost gone, man."

She blinked. "How?"

"I'll put on some kick butt tunes and light the sage. We'll dance. Chase him out. You on board?"

"Why would we dance?" Myra gulped.

"Ghosts hate music. Sage cleans the space."

"I don't dance," she said bluntly.

"That's okay. You can move your arms," he said, with a wink and another grin.

"We get the sage. We've done that a couple of times." I interrupted the two. "I'll dance." Myra looked uncomfortable. Her jaw was tight and her shoulders tensed as if she might bolt.

I'd do a jig if it meant getting rid of the ghost. I felt

guilty that Myra had bought the house from me, ghost included, before we knew the land was haunted. To be fair, once upon a time the dwelling had been in her family, so she wasn't totally in the dark. Dancing was the least I could do.

"Ready?" Bernie loaded the disc player. It was surreal as the theme song from the old movie blared, "Ghostbusters!"

I rolled my shoulders, getting into the rhythm. Myra, her face stoic, lightly lifted her hands and swayed with the music. I did the moon walk, à la Michael Jackson. Bernie shook his head in the manner of a head banger, and swiveled his hips, enjoying the momentum. Suddenly, we heard "Awaaaaill" in a tortured tone. "Awaaaaaill."

There was a puff of smoke from the planting bed beside the old garage. Myra gasped. The music player went silent. We quit dancing.

"Did we do it? Is the spirit gone for good?" I whispered.

Bernie winked and grinned. "Yep. Might be. We'll light the sage now."

"Oh," Myra said, inhaling. "Is that necessary?" Her complexion had paled with a greenish cast. I felt a little sick to my stomach, too.

"Best to be thorough. We'll start with the spot where the smoke appeared, then trek the edge of the lot," Bernie said, his voice a high tenor. The traffic was picking up. The Hiptown lot was a street over from the main drag, and the sounds from vehicles threatened our mission.

He dug out the sage bundles and plates. Lighting each bunch, he handed them off. "We'd better hurry."

"Amen," I said, and hurriedly crossed myself. Myra hesitated, then did the same. The ghostbuster led the way to the garage spot, holding the plate with the sage above his head, the smoke wafting into the area.

I mimicked his movements, and Myra sighed, following suit. One by one, we marched with a container of sage held high around the border of the grounds. When we finished the perimeter, the ghostbuster motioned to the home's foundation, where the footings were ready for the cement pour. Myra and I glanced at each other and followed him as he rounded the area and stopped at the garage site.

"Done." Bernie blew out his bundle. We quickly snuffed out our packets.

"Everything all right?" An early morning runner called. He'd stopped en route to the lake. Dressed in a gray t-shirt, shorts, and wearing a cap to shield his eyes from the dawning sun, he stretched his muscular legs while he observed us.

"We're good!" I yelled. Myra nodded.

"Thanks, man!" Bernie bobbed in agreement. He collected our plates and the remaining sage, stashed the dishes in his pack, zipped up, slipped the pack on his back, and hoisted the boom box.

The runner surveyed our group. We must have been a spectacle, even for the jaded city dwellers of Hiptown.

"Okay." He shrugged and ran off.

"So, we're done?" I asked Bernie, ghostbuster, Lyft driver, and marriage officiator.

"Yep." He stood and said loud enough for any passersby, his head bobbing, "Your space is clear. This place is gonna be awesome!"

Myra and I looked at each other.

"How can you be so sure?" Myra asked.

"Everything is as it is. You are where you are." Myra handed him a check and, loaded with his wares, he strolled to the sidewalk, and sauntered across the street to the lakeside path. The sun rose higher in the sky and robins chirped. We watched his back until he disappeared.

"What does that mean?" I burst out, laughing.

"Who knows?" Myra sniffed, her brows creased, and she scanned the lot. "It seems better." It was brighter with the sunlight filtering through the trees to the site. The air smelled fresh. The day was warming.

"You know. It does." I cocked my head and studied the site. "I'm sure it will be a great home!"

"I think so, too. Like Bernie said, 'It'll be awesome!'"

"Our job is complete," I said, and gave her a light hug. "I'm off to the flip." My newest renovation project was an easy-peasy, cosmetic refresh in my old stomping grounds of Crocus Heights, Minnesota. I wanted less traffic and drama after the Hiptown project had gone up in flames.

"I'm meeting with the contractor for the new house," Myra said, and checked her watch. "Oops. I'd better go."

"Good luck!"

She waved and hurried to her black SUV parked on the street overlooking the "couples" lake in Minneapolis.

I lingered, scanning the lot for the new construction. *I hope this does the trick.*

Mulling over Myra's new building project, I headed to my white hatchback, eager to start my newest project.

Flipping homes is how I make my living since I quit my job at the hospital. Okay, maybe it was mutual. Well, maybe it was more their idea than mine. I won't bore you with the details, except to say it wasn't pretty.

Rehabbing houses has been more challenging than I'd expected, but this new project on Warbler Street promised to be peaceful. Until later that day.

Chapter 1

"Oh dang, not again!" Boots, my Tuxedo cat, surveyed me coolly from his perch on the counter while he licked his paws. "Easy for you to say. Remember what happened at Hiptown?" He wrinkled his nose. Like the old comedian said, I get no respect.

I watched the ambulance, police, and fire rescue activity from the picture window. Rescue workers walked a gurney out of the home across the street to the waiting ambulance. They'd covered the form on the transport from head to toe with a sheet. The EMTs loaded the body while two officers talked to the homeowner.

"Boots, stay here while I check it out." I dropped my broom and trotted outside, lingering on my lawn with two others who'd ventured out to see what had transpired. The officers were talking to Fernando Garcia, the jovial, happy-go-lucky homeowner I'd met while evaluating the split-level dwelling on Warbler Street.

"I think Sarah had been ill," a woman chimed. "That's her husband. The handsome, bronzed-skinned man. He's very friendly. She kept her maiden name, Anderson." She was a chatty, fiftyish, plump gal who lived in a tidy rambler next to my split. I'd seen her out mowing her lawn and walking a small white dog."

"I saw blood on the sheet," another neighbor, a man, said.

"Oh my!" The talkative woman gasped and the three

of us stared.

I spotted Don Williams, the local sheriff and my reluctant love interest pulling up in his squad. He leaped out, the silver in his blond hair catching the light, shoulders squared, and jaw firm, as he joined the officers and husband of the deceased. I left the neighbors on the lawn, caught Don's eye, and moved in closer.

"She was being treated for vertigo. I came home from work for lunch and found her in the kitchen. There was blood all over. I called 9-1-1. I don't know what happened," the dark-eyed husband recounted. His attitude had been open and disarming when we met, but he shook now, wiped his brow, and blotted his face with a handkerchief taken from his back pocket.

"The medical examiner will determine the cause of death. Until then, the residence is a crime scene. Let the detectives do their job," Don said. "We'll need you to come to the station for an interview." Two men escorted the distraught spouse to a squad and drove away. The ambulance left the scene, the sirens silent.

By this time, I stood next to the sheriff.

"Katelyn. You again," he said with a brief smirk.

"I always show up wherever there's a dead body," I snarked. I was peeved about our standoffish relationship. It didn't help that I found him great looking, albeit aloof. I gave him credit for showing up with an apology pizza the last time he'd visited. It was the least he could do when he was interested in someone else. Or so I thought. He'd never explained the perky redhead he'd been with and said it was best if we were just "friends." Yeah. Right.

Just then the white sewer/drain cleaning truck I'd seen a few times roared past, throwing up dust as it rumbled through the neighborhood. Randy's Plumbing truck advertised his business with a picture of a leaking faucet on the side panels.

Lord, please don't let me have any water problems.

"Are you okay?" The sheriff watched as I paled with the silent prayer. My last flip had been a nightmare with water complications, and the mere presence of a plumber made me squeamish. Not to mention the resident spirits that had made the renovation untenable.

"I'm fine. What happened?"

"We're investigating the woman's death," he said. "Why are you here?"

I pointed to the split-level. "It's my newest project. A creampuff. A little cleanup, painting, and flooring replacement. It has a newer roof. The original siding has been updated to vinyl. No maintenance," I crowed.

"You bought a rehab in a neighborhood where a death just occurred." His eyebrows shot up and he gave me a weary glance.

"Hey. Just what are you saying?" I stood my ground and stared him down. I'm sure my hair was a full-blown, dark brown disaster, and I probably had dirt on my face from sweeping out the garage.

"Harrumph." The lines at the corners of his eyes crinkled. "You have a penchant for being in the wrong place at the wrong time." He stared at the renovation. The place looked dismal. The lawn needed mowing, and the bushes begged trimming. Everything needed cleaning. My old, but spunky Ford Festiva in the driveway needed a car wash too.

"I resent that," I sputtered.

"Where's Wayne?" he asked. "Doesn't he help with your rehabs?" Wayne Hamer is my handyman.

"Visiting his daughter in Michigan. He took Gillie with him." The two seniors had been seeing a lot of each other, and it wouldn't surprise me if they made it permanent. Gillie, or Mrs. Greta Gilman, had challenged his attitude towards commitment, and it looked as if they might make it a legal union. Both are my neighbors at the townhouses where I live.

"You're working alone?" He frowned. "No Myra?"

"She's at the Hiptown house. I can handle myself, and I have my cat for company." Boots, my rescue cat, is a good listener, but not so good at conversing.

I took a deep breath and gestured toward the ranch-style house from where the woman had been removed. "Do you think she was murdered?" I asked, alarmed.

He dodged my question, and his gaze narrowed. "So, Wayne and Gillie are away?"

"Crocus Heights is a safe area," I protested. My heart warmed with the thought that Don Williams worried about my working alone, and being at home without neighbors nearby.

"You know," he said, and he focused laser eyes on mine, "bad things happen in good neighborhoods, too."

"Great," I muttered under my breath.

"Be aware of your surroundings. Keep your doors locked. Take normal precautions." He relaxed, and chuckled. "I know you can handle yourself. Boots is no slouch, either." The cat had come to my defense and attacked a bad guy from my last project, causing the creep much pain and many scratches.

"This part of town has an abundance of wildlife. Watch out for owls. We've had reports of the birds attacking cats and small dogs."

"Owls?" I was incredulous.

"A female owl will attack if she feels threatened. Especially when protecting her young," Don said. "Great horned owls can attack small mammals."

"Is that so?" I glanced toward the backyard, which was bordered by a large wooded lot. The residence was on a path to the river, full of mice and small animals that the creatures like for food.

"Yep. They're fierce. They're called the Tigers of

the Air," Don said. "It's their nesting season and they may have a new brood. Their talons are dangerous weapons if they're riled."

It was late March. Snow was still possible. April rains would clean up the crusted remains of the winter landscape, if Mother Nature didn't dump more of the white stuff.

"I'll watch out for owls. When will we know anything about the death?" I asked, gesturing towards the neighbor's residence. Crime scene tape was stretched across the door.

"There is no 'we,' Katelyn. The only person who needs to know is the husband," he said firmly.

"This could affect my resale value, if the death isn't natural or an accident," I protested. "I'm not being snoopy."

"Uh huh." He viewed me, skeptically. "The authorities will investigate. It's best you get back to work."

"Friends is just fine with me," I grumbled, as I left. "Just fine."

"What did you say?" he called as I reached the edge of my property.

"Nothing." I grimaced and shrugged. I wouldn't let the sheriff get the better of me. I'd had a decent day at the job. I'd made a dent in cleaning and prepared a list of repairs. Boots had been a fabulous, albeit quiet, companion. It worried me it wasn't a slam dunk that the woman died of natural causes. I'd keep an eye on the handsome husband, and be alert for owls. It's the spouse who has the most to gain financially when a wife dies, and I'd make a point of talking to him, if only to satisfy my curiosity.

I went inside and gathered my cleaning supplies and equipment, and stored them in a corner for the next day's work, then coaxed Boots into his carrier.

"Let's get some chow." I grabbed my messenger bag, and headed home. It was dinnertime, and I was famished. My lunch was a snack, and I'd kept going all day fortified by strong coffee.

The exterior of my four-unit complex resembles a stately English Tudor-style residence, with a stucco finish and wood beams as accents. Besides the appeal of looking like a single-family dwelling, the central hall entrance has the added benefit of sheltering each unit entry from rain and snow.

"Oh, oh." I spotted Eddy Pascal's pickup in the parking lot as I drove up and parked in my garage. He wasn't in his truck, which meant he let himself in.

Eddy is renting my Bluebird Street rehab and has a habit of showing up, calling me "Wifey" to annoy me, and saying weird stuff, like, "We could get married again." We'd married as teenagers, divorced after a year of fighting, but remained friends.

Later, I'd married Jake, and lost him. I tell most people he died in an accident, cleaner that way. Saying he'd died saving the life of a youngster who'd been playing with his cell phone while walking on railroad tracks is too much information, until you get to know someone.

Life with Eddy was always a surprise. Like when he lost jobs, or got another one, or took up with a woman, and left that one for another. He meant well, but his follow-through wasn't always the best.

I stopped at the letterboxes outside the homes and plucked out the mail for Wayne, Mrs. Gilman, and myself. I'd promised to collect the mail for the couple while they were on vacation. When I reached my door, the first unit, I took a deep breath and went in.

"Katie!" Eddy chortled from his sprawled position on the sofa. He had a remote in one hand, a beer in the other. His deep brown eyes danced, and I treaded warily. Boots yowled from his cage while I unloaded the mail and my bag on the kitchen table.

"Let me help." He leaped up, grabbed the crate and opened it. The cat darted to his bowls, and meowed again when he saw they were empty.

"What's up? The key is for emergencies." I couldn't help nagging, and bit my tongue to stop a torrent of questions.

"Katie, I wanted you to be the first to know." He sidled in beside me while I took out a can of kitty chow from the kitchen cupboard.

"Know what?"

"Lola and I are getting back together. She's moving in with me."

I dropped the can. It clattered and rolled off the counter. I lunged for it; he caught it first. Handing over the tin, he grinned, and his eyes sparkled.

"Here. You dropped this."

"Yeah, yeah." My stomach had made an unexpected lurch, but I recovered. "So, you want to put her on the lease?"

"No. Don't need to. I thought you'd want to know."

"I'm happy for you, Eddy." As a couple, we'd been over long ago, but no one was more surprised than me at my reaction. Somehow, I thought he'd always be there. A slightly annoying, but constant presence.

"You look a little green," he countered.

"It's been a rough day. They took the woman who lived across the street from my Warbler Street project out on a gurney, dead." I paused in opening the container.

"No!" His eyes widened. "What happened?"

"Don't know. One neighbor said she'd been sick, another reported he'd seen blood on the sheet covering her. The husband claims she had vertigo."

"Vertigo doesn't bleed, Kate," he said, grimly.

"No. But, if she had a dizzy spell and fell, she might have banged her head. That would explain the blood," I suggested.

"Yeah. That's rough," he said. "The husband found her?"

"Yes." I nodded, while dishing food into the cat's bowl.

"Do you want me to stay? We could get a pizza? Your choice?" He leaned against the counter, his arms crossed and gazed expectantly. He knew my weakness for Hawaiian pizza.

"No. I'm sure Lola's waiting for you." I placed the cat's bowl, and filled the water dish.

"She's not like that. She's cool."

"Huh." I glanced at him. I didn't know what he meant and didn't care to ask. "I'll see you out." I pushed him towards the exit. "Thanks for telling me about Lola."

"No problem, wifey." He grinned and held his hand to his mouth. "Sorry, it slipped out."

I shut the door and did an eye-roll. I headed to the refrigerator, rummaging for dinner, fixed a peanut butter sandwich, poured a glass of wine, and placed the laptop on the table by the plate. I had to distract myself from Eddy's news. Learning that he and Lola were getting back together had sent me into a funk. Things would change, and probably affect our rental agreement. Not to mention, he wouldn't be as available for the occasional favor where muscle was needed.

As the machine powered up, I shook my head at Boots who stared at me after scarfing his chow.

"What are you looking at? I'm not snooping!" I started Googling the neighbor who lived across from my newest property. After searching for some time, I got fed up with dead ends. Although I knew his name as

Fernando Garcia and his wife as Sarah Anderson, both names were common. She'd kept her maiden name, so she wasn't traditional in the sense of taking her husband's surname. I gave up, powered down the computer, and went to bed.

I'd have to rely on old-fashioned, in-person snooping.

My credentials for private investigating are sketchy. I credit myself with being nosy and determined. And maybe sneaky.

Chapter 2

The next morning, I started work by ripping up worn carpet in the main living area of the split entry. The sun was rising with rays of orange and yellow. I brought Boots again, deciding he could have the run of the place. He lounged on the kitchen counter while I worked and spied on Fernando's residence.

My mission was to track the neighbor's movements. A dead wife is a hot button for me. After all, I'd been a wife a couple of times. Granted, neither Eddy nor Jake had tried to do away with me, but relationships can be frustrating. Was Sarah's death natural? An accident? Or something more sinister?

Okay, snooping kept my mind off something too painful to admit. I was lonely. Eddy getting back with Lola had reminded me I was unattached. Single. Don was distant and unavailable. I missed the companionable silence that Wayne and I had as we worked. Myra was preoccupied with building the new residence in Hiptown. Any restless spirits must be at rest, because I hadn't heard from her. Roy Orbison's tune of "Only the Lonely" alternating with Adele's "Rolling in the Deep" rumbled in my mind, and added to the solitary feeling.

FWEET FEW! The cell phone broke my funk with a wolf whistle tone, and I fumbled for it in the pocket of my hoodie. I'd changed the sound out of desperation for entertainment. Besides, the catcall made me feel pretty.

Lunch at Ivan's? the text read. It was Myra. Ivan had dropped the Popov's surname from the diner's name for the sake of simplicity. He also thought it lent the grill an upscale air, something Maggie, his wife, longed for.

Sounds good. 1:00?

See you there.

The exchange lifted my spirits. At last, a friendly voice. I went back to the job at hand. The project was moving along. Thank goodness for the mini-crowbar. Using the tool, I lifted the room's molding and pulled the carpet from the padding. Removing the pad and pulling staples from the subfloor would be the next chore. Systematically, I folded the rug back and ripped it with a carpet knife, tearing it into manageable sections. I'd ordered a roll-off dumpster to haul away the waste, which I expected to be delivered that morning.

Periodically, I'd stop and peer at the neat, sienna-colored, ranch-style dwelling with stone accents. It looked like a solid starter home. I presumed the owners were going for a tropical or desert feel with the color.

Between my carpet removal and surveillance of the neighbor's residence, the rubbish hauler arrived and backed into the driveway. I watched from the front door as he left the container. The driver waved and drove away. Propping the door open, I began hauling old flooring to the dumpster. A flash of black and white fur dashed past me.

"BOOTS. NO! Dang it anyway!" Exasperated, I sprinted after the cat.

He picked up speed and darted to a maple tree. I charged after him. He passed on the maple and darted to the base of the next tree.

"No," I pleaded. "Boots. NO!" Giving me a sly look, he put paws up, ready to climb a red oak. From out of nowhere a huge bird swooped down, talons extended.

"NOOOOOO!" I screamed and waved my arms, hyperventilating.

The great horned owl retracted its claws, and its wings brushed the rebel cat, startling him. I gasped and held my breath. Boots yowled, turned tail and sprinted into the house. "Serves you right, silly cat," I chided and strode to the entry, my face flushed, agitated from the close encounter.

"You must be mindful of the owls. Particularly in the early morning. The noise from the waste hauler delivering the dumpster must have disturbed it." The silky voice startled me and I jumped. It was Fernando, his face creased with worry. "They have new babies to feed." He wore jeans and a navy hoodie and gripped a mug of coffee. The aroma of fresh java wafted towards me.

"I guess." My adrenaline was up. I caught my breath and brushed back unruly hair. I hadn't spoken with him since the first time I viewed the Warbler Street project, before his wife's death. Remembering my manners, I said, "I'm sorry about your wife."

"Yes. Thank you." He nodded; his face fell. Saddened, he turned towards his house. He stopped and pivoted, his brown eyes dim. "Forgive me. It's been a shock."

"Of course." I nodded with sympathy. He didn't look like a killer, and I had a pang of guilt about my earlier surveillance. He was so vulnerable in his grief.

"How is your remodel coming? Your flip, I believe it is called?" An accent colored his questions. His face brightened with interest.

"The project is going well. I should have the living room carpet out today."

"I would be happy to help? It is heavy work." He grinned with an engaging attitude but his eyes were still sad.

"No. Thank you. I'm fine. I need the exercise," I joked. I bit my tongue, thinking this was a bad time to kid, and added, "I do a lot of demolition work."

"It is my pleasure. Perhaps I could dispose of a few

items in the container? I would help with your flip in exchange?"

"Well, in that case, that'd be great. But are you sure you have time?" I asked delicately.

"Sarah had made plans for her passing," he said, understanding the meaning behind my question. He sighed. "She had been ill for some time."

"Oh?" I was puzzled. Vertigo didn't seem serious.

"She had many health problems. She suffered with depression and high blood pressure. The doctors were trying to control her health problems with different drugs. The dizzy spells were caused by the medications she took." He rubbed his temple, as if he relived the confusion of Sarah's health symptoms.

A case of the cure being worse than the disease.

"I'm sorry," I nodded, empathetic. After all, I'd lost Jake, my husband and love of my life.

"Thank you." He lowered his gaze, and said quietly, "My Sarah had two boxes she wanted to dump or donate."

"You don't have a garbage service?" I frowned, hesitating. My thoughts went on overdrive. Why would Fernando dispose of his wife's belongings so fast?

"It is embarrassing." He flushed. "We share a service with a family member's business. But two boxes are too much. We have one bag a week. Many times, it is not a full bag."

"Okay." I scratched my head.

"Sarah had many medical bills. We saved money by sharing trash removal," he explained.

"You won't have to pay anything. Let's call it neighborly," I said, thinking quickly. That made sense. But my suspicions rose again. "Why not donate?"

"It would save a trip to the thrift store and be most convenient."

So, time and gas money. He had medical bills and

now funeral bills. I understood his thrifty ways. I kept my expression bland, dismissing any doubt about ulterior motives, and said, "I'm going to lunch. Knock yourself out."

"Thank you very much." He smiled, and the sun glowed brighter. He was indeed very handsome. His mood had lightened during our exchange and I left with another guilty twinge.

I met Myra at our favorite restaurant, Ivan's Bar and Grill, at 1 p.m. Ivan and Maggie stood at their usual spot at the front of the restaurant, greeting customers as they arrived.

"Good to see you!" Ivan grinned and Maggie chimed, "Ya!" They were Russian immigrants, and their speech was colored with the accent of their native country.

"Hi, Ivan, Maggie." I nodded. I smiled at Myra, who waited by the hostess station. I was flushed from my conversation with Fernando and his request to use my dumpster, not to mention Boot's close encounter with the owl. I'd thrown a jacket over my sweatshirt and jeans, smoothed my hair and dabbed on lipstick to meet Myra. Despite her own project in Hiptown, she looked calm, cool, collected, and sported a new hairstyle. If we weren't good friends, it would be annoying. As it was, I tried to take more care with my fashion-challenged style. I try. Honest.

Our not-so-favorite hostess, Katarina, seated us in a booth in view of the dish bussing station and dropped menus. "I bring you coffee!" She stalked off. Her shoulders were squared and a bad attitude seeped from every pore.

"She's got to be family," I whispered, staring at her rigid posture.

"Must be," Myra murmured. "Ivan says he wants to

go upscale."

"Really? In Crocus Heights?" I shrugged, doubtful.

"It might be a nice change," she said, and smiled.

"Hum," I said, not convinced. In a rush, and with a low voice, I said, "I have news about the neighbor who lives across from my rehab."

"Do you mean the husband of the woman who died?" She lowered her menu and looked at me, eyebrows furrowed. I'd filled her in on Fernando.

"Yes. He wants to dispose of boxes from his deceased wife." I was breathless, flushed with the news. "In my dumpster! And an owl almost took Boots!"

"He's throwing away his wife's belongings?" She laid down her menu, immediately attentive. "That seems quick, and rather odd." She frowned. "They've wrapped up the investigation at his house?"

"I thought it was fast too. Yes, they removed all the crime scene tape."

"I guess that would be fine, if they're done. But to get rid of his wife's things the same day seems questionable."

"He said she'd packed two boxes, planning to donate or throw them before she died."

"That is different." She cocked her head. "They aren't containers that he packed?"

"No. He says she did."

"How can you be sure he's telling you the truth?" Her expression was searching, and she tilted her head, pensive.

"I can't. When it gets dark, I'm going to take out the cases, and go through them," I whispered, excited.

The server appeared at my elbow. "You order now!" and I jumped.

Myra and I looked at each other, stifled snickers, and chose the Ivan burgers, one of their specialties.

"What happened with Boots?" she asked and sipped

her coffee.

"A huge owl rushed him. He ran out as I was taking the old carpet to the trash container. It scared me to death."

"I'll bet."

"I yelled so loud the bird flew away." I laughed.

"Good for you!" She inhaled and grinned.

"Yep. I think my screams brought Fernando out of his house. He's very handsome." A flush of color warmed my face. I reached for my coffee and cradled the warm cup in both hands.

"I wish I could be there," Myra said, and studied me. By then, my face felt crimson. She sat back. "Handsome? You do remember his wife just died? Under dubious circumstances?"

"Yep." Yikes, what was I thinking? "I think I need to get out more," I added lamely.

"You do," she nodded, and went on, "I'm so busy with the new house in Hiptown, it'll be months before I have any free time."

"How's the construction coming?" I asked, eager to change the subject.

"Frustrating." She shrugged; her expression dimmed. "New construction is a big job. I needed a breather from the turmoil."

"What's going on?" I frowned, noting her normally relaxed voice sounded clipped, her face clouded.

"The lumber delivery was late, so the framers were idle. The contractor was mad." She shook her head, disgusted. "It's a mess."

"Oh boy. Makes my project look easy. Sorry." I winced. "At least there aren't any spirits?"

"No. They've left. The ghostbuster's ritual was a success." She smiled briefly and shook her head. "I know it'll all work out." She pushed her plate away, her hazel eyes twinkling, "But now you have a mystery with the dead neighbor."

"We'll see," I said, mulling over the situation with Fernando and his deceased wife.

"Let me know if you find out anything interesting," she said as she raised her brows, a hint of laughter in her expression.

"You'll be the first to know," I promised.

FWEET FEW!

Myra jumped, gasping. "What was that?"

"My new texting sound. It makes me feel cute," I protested and batted my eyelashes. I dug the phone out of my pocket and glanced at the screen. "It's Eddy. I'll call him later."

"You should change that sound. What if it goes off in the woman's restroom?" she sniffed.

"Not the best time for a catcall," I conceded.

"No, it isn't," she said, crossing her arms.

Katerina came back. "I leave you check!" She dropped our tickets and stomped away.

"We've got to find another place to eat," I said. With a sigh, I reached in my handbag for cash.

"Let's see what happens when Ivan goes upscale," Myra laughed. We left money for the tab and slid from the booth.

After lunch, I pulled up to the rehab and parked by the dumpster. I peered inside the container, checking for Fernando's boxes. Nothing yet. I went inside to face Boots.

"Yowl!" His greeting was disdainful, with green eyes narrowed, and tail held high, he scolded me.

"Okay, this isn't your cup of tea. Tomorrow, I'll leave you at home." I kneeled to stroke the cat, and he meowed an agreement. "Getting rushed by a huge bird isn't fun." I shuddered to think what could have happened, and was happy the cat had escaped.

I tackled the floor covering again, sporadically looking through the window. I stopped in the middle of shredding when I saw Fernando trek from his house carrying a cardboard box and tossing it into the dumpster, then he returned with another one, chucking it. He saw that I watched from the picture window and waved.

Curses, caught in the act.

I brushed hair from my face and went out to meet him at the rear of the container. “Hi, should be plenty of room,” I said, “even with pitching two floors of carpeting.”

“I appreciate this, Katelyn.” His expression was serious.

“No problem. Have you heard anything from the police?”

“No. It is difficult. I miss her every minute of the day.” His face clouded, and he brushed his hands on his jeans.

“I’m sure you do.” I could relate.

“Thank you for your understanding. The police are not as kind when they ask me about my Sarah.” He smiled softly, his eyes shined, and his shoulders relaxed. “They are just doing their job. I am a suspect, her partner, and I found her.” He shrugged. “They ask many questions. It is troubling.”

“The spouse is usually the first suspect, if there is foul play,” I agreed. “How did you meet her?” It seemed unlikely the grief-stricken man had done anything to his wife.

“I met my Sarah in Arizona. She was the love of my life.”

“You were married for a long time?”

“We were committed to each other for a short while, a year.” He smiled sadly. “We were both married before. They were not happy unions, and we felt blessed we found each other."

"It is hard losing someone you love." The words slipped out. I told myself that I was a professional Home Rehab Specialist. I would keep mum about personal information until I was positive that Fernando wasn't responsible for his wife's demise. But under his friendly, compassionate gaze, I'd nearly blurted out my life's story.

"We should have coffee sometime?" he asked. His gaze caressed my face. My color heightened, and I saw again his vulnerability. He was lonely, too.

"Uh, sure." Mentally, I kicked myself and muttered, "I have to go," and darted inside, with my stomach churning and shoulders shaking. Despite my reservations about his guilt, I found him attractive. Sighing, I slapped the side of my head, composed myself, and tore into the job at hand. The adrenaline from my encounter propelled my efforts, and I tore out the carpeting with renewed vigor. On my last trip of the day to the container, I placed a piece of flooring over the boxes Fernando had thrown, but kept them accessible to dumpster diving later.

My eagerness at telling Myra that I'd steal the containers out was dimmed by the thought it was a dead end. Would a guilty husband really dispose of evidence that could easily be traced to him? He'd likely seen the sheriff and me together while his wife's body was removed. The cases were probably filled with odds and ends.

I corralled Boots into his crate, grabbed my purse, and trekked to my car, motoring out. It was about four o'clock. Darkness comes early in March. Later, I could sneak back to retrieve the containers. With any luck, Fernando would be asleep, and I'd get the items without his knowledge. That was the plan, anyway. I drove away, noting that he'd parked his red truck in his driveway and didn't appear to use the detached garage.

At home, my telephone jangled as I burst through the door. Dropping the cat's crate and my handbag, I answered, breathless.

"Hey, Kiddo!" the handyman's voice declared. Wayne always called me "Kiddo." It had been his nickname for me from the beginning of our friendship.

"Wayne! How are you? I miss you! Are you having fun in Michigan? When will you and Gillie be back? You were thinking next week?"

"Got a change of plans." he chuckled.

"What's up?" I asked.

"Gillie and I are going to Vegas."

"Vegas?" I paused, letting the information sink in. "As in Las Vegas, the marriage capital of the world?"

"Yep!" He let out a guffaw. "We're gonna have us a commitment ceremony!"

"Oh Wayne." I heard Gillie's voice in the background. "You and Mrs. Gilman are getting married?" I'd have to remember to call Mrs. Gilman Gillie, or even Greta, her first name. I was dumbfounded at Wayne's news.

"Sort of." He chuckled.

"What do you mean?" I asked.

"We're having a commitment ceremony, not a marriage ceremony."

"I'm confused." I frowned. "Isn't it the same idea?"

"Yeah, I was, too. But it's pretty simple. The commitment ceremony says we're committed to each other, but not legally married."

"Huh?"

"Yep. The chapel does a ceremony, vows, the whole deal. Then we get a copy of Elvis' marriage document, signifying Gillie and me have a commitment."

"And, she's okay with that?"

"Heck yeah. She said I was 'commitment' phobic. This is gonna put that problem to rest!"

I had my doubts about whether Gillie would be satisfied with the vows, without a marriage license, but I said, "I wish you both the best."

"Thanks, Kiddo!"

"So, when do you think you'll be back?" Most of the repairs I could manage without Wayne, but there were some that I couldn't, like framing out the mirror in the main bathroom, or changing out plumbing fixtures. I didn't have the strength and skill that Wayne did, and relied on him.

"Haven't decided. How's the new rehab? Sorry, I ain't there."

"The rehab's good. No worries. Take as much time as you need. You two should have the time of your lives." I wanted the seniors to make the most of their trip. I'd tackle what I could by myself.

"It's gonna be fantastic! There're all kinds of shows and we're pumped about Elvis and the ceremony!"

"That's great, Wayne."

I signed off from the handyman, unhappy at the prospect of continuing the rehab by myself, and consoled myself with Googling Fernando. I thought about how much he missed his wife and the cartons he'd discarded. The silence of the townhomes without the comings and goings of my friends and neighbors made me a little stir crazy. I considered returning to the rehab.

"Enough of this." I powered down the computer. "I'll get the boxes now, before the garbage hauler does." Boots yawned, licked a paw and curled up on the sofa.

I showered and threw on black jeans, a sweater and a black jacket, finishing the outfit with a black stocking cap. Maybe it was overkill, but I didn't want to be seen.

I had a house under renovation, so it wouldn't be unusual for me to be there, but I wanted to do anything possible, to be invisible.

It was ten o'clock, long after darkness fell, when I headed back to the renovation.

Chapter 3

I parked in the driveway beside the dumpster, killed the engine and headlights, and slipped out into the murky night. The rehab was set back from the street on a generous-sized lot. I'd nearly bypassed the dwelling because that part of the block had no street lights. The neighborhood was asleep except for an occasional flicker of a television screen or a porch light.

"Hoot, hoot." The great horned owls nesting in the nearby woods were awake and hunting for prey. I stilled my breath and walked to the end of the container where I'd placed carpet over the cartons Fernando had dumped. I glanced over at his place, spotted his truck parked in the drive, and the lights out. He was asleep.

I reached over the side and pushed the carpet aside. Jumping up, I grabbed the cardboard box by the top flaps. Pulling it closer, I grunted, lifting the carton over the edge of the dumpster. It slipped from my hands and tumbled to the ground.

"Dang it!" I gathered the spillage, stuffing the contents back in the box. There were papers and photo albums, which heightened my curiosity. Lights went on inside of Fernando's place. I ducked by the roll-off container and held my breath. I waited, wondering if he would come out. After what seemed an eternity, the lights went off. I gathered my courage and carried the box to the hatch of my car.

After I stashed the carton in the back, I considered waiting on the second box, and decided there was no time like the present. I returned to the dumpster. Making the same maneuvers, I hopped up and grabbed the flaps of the last carton. Resting the container on the edge, a quick peek inside revealed clothing. I toted it to the back of the car, stowed it, and slammed the hatch.

"Roo roo roo!" the siren of an unmarked police car sounded, the lights flashed, and the vehicle halted behind my car. I stopped in my tracks. A few lights went on in neighboring houses.

"Katelyn, is that you?" Sheriff Don Williams leaned his head out of the driver's side window. The lights from the car blinded me and his tone was firm.

"Yes! You got me," I exhaled and faced him, throwing up my hands in a lame joke.

He dimmed the headlights. His face was lit from interior lights of the squad. He was not amused. He examined me with a stern gaze, and his mouth tightened.

"Is there a problem? I was checking on my investment property." I figured my best defense was a good offense.

"Someone reported a prowler."

"Who called?"

"Doesn't matter. It's late to be working at the rehab, isn't it? Are you alone?"

"Yes. I'm alone." I wished people would quit reminding me. "House renovations go on at all hours of the night. For cripes' sake, I'm not making noise or creating a disturbance!"

"No need to get testy, Katelyn. Here, the neighbors watch for prowlers or unusual activity; they look out for each other and the neighborhood. Makes the area safer."

"Yes. You're right," I agreed. "I couldn't remember if I'd locked up." I crossed my fingers, hoping he hadn't noticed my voice getting higher with the little white lie. "What are you doing? Doesn't the sheriff have regular daytime hours?"

"I'm covering for another officer. He had a family

emergency."

"Okay. I couldn't recall, and it bugged me. So, I'm checking. That's all there is to it." I kept my fingers crossed.

Silently, he studied me, and I felt my face burn. "This wouldn't have anything to do with the woman who was found dead, would it?"

"What do you mean?" I was on the defensive.

"Are you spying? Trying to figure out what Fernando Garcia is doing at night? Inserting yourself into a police investigation?"

"Don't be silly. I was just about to leave. If you'd move your car, I'll back out."

"I'll follow you." He sat behind the wheel and watched closely. He flipped off the interior lights. "We need to talk. Now is not the time, but soon."

"All right." Did he want to give me a longer lecture? My knees jelly and face crimson, I huffed and slid in the driver's seat, slamming the door. Don backed out. He shadowed me to my townhouse. I obeyed all the rules of the road, trying to still my panic attack at being caught looting my own dumpster. There could be something in the cartons the police would want, but here I was, absconding with potential evidence. When would I learn?

The sheriff remained in his car while I parked in the garage. He waited until I entered the corridor. Once I was inside, he sped off.

I waited a few minutes, then trekked back to the car, dug out the two boxes and lugged them inside.

Out of breath, I dropped the last container.

"Thank goodness I have you, Boots." He yowled for a treat. I gave him a nibble, and he scampered to his favorite spot on the sofa. I slipped off my stocking cap and jacket and warmed a cup of coffee in the microwave.

While the coffee heated, I dialed Myra. I flinched; it was after eleven. It was late to be calling. But I needed a welcoming voice, outside of the comfort of the cat's purrs. Eddy was probably awake, but he was with Lola, and I didn't want to shake that tree. Wayne and Gillie were in Vegas, likely celebrating their commitment vows.

"What's up?" Her sleepy voice answered on the third ring. In my opinion, the genuine test of a friend is whether they take your calls, no matter what time of the day or night. Myra had been tested often during our dozen or so years of friendship, and she always picked up.

"Whoopee! I've got the cartons Fernando discarded in my dumpster," I chortled, giddy with excitement.

"You're kidding!" She sounded fully awake.

"I wouldn't joke about possible evidence. You know what else?"

"What?"

"Don practically caught me dumpster diving. Someone reported a prowler, and they must've seen me. I almost fainted!"

"Really? It may have been an actual lurker. You were at the house?"

"Yes, at the renovation."

"You own the property," she said. "You have every right to be there."

"But it's not occupied."

"True enough. What now?"

"I'm going to search the boxes!" I chortled.

"I wish I could be there," she groaned. "I have an early morning appointment with the contractor."

"That's all right. I just needed to hear a kind voice and a little support."

"You have it! I'll expect a full report tomorrow."

"Thanks, Myra." With her blessing, I sipped coffee

and started going through the cases. I dove into the container that had spilled out papers and photographs. The papers were a mishmash of receipts from paid telephone and utility bills.

Who keeps this kind of stuff? I frowned at the collection of receipts. The pictures were more interesting. They showed Sarah in an earlier lifetime with another man. *Must be her first husband?* I shoved the stuff back inside. Frustrated, I sat back on my heels. No mystery that she'd dump this stuff. The real mystery was why she'd save this stuff at all. Fernando had said both of their early marriages had been unhappy, and they felt blessed to find each other. Why had she kept the mementos?

I dug into the next box and whistled.

"Hello, the nineties called, and they want their shoulder pads back." Sarah must have been a compulsive saver. There were blazers, sweaters, and dresses with massive shoulder pads, a hallmark of the 80s and 90s. A tea-length, oyster-white dress was wadded into a ball concealing two champagne flutes. I rummaged around in the box. "Ouch!" I felt a nick on my finger, withdrew my hand, and saw drops of blood.

"Dang." I ran to the kitchen for a paper towel and blotted the blood. After slapping on a Band-Aid, I rifled through the contents of the carton and pulled out the culprit, a fancy pie-shaped serving knife and wide fork. I wrinkled my nose. "Yikes, these look lethal." They were likely remnants of her early, unhappy marriage. I cleaned the fork and knife and put the items back, wrapping them in a 90s-style tweed blazer.

If there were any clues, it would take a full-fledged detective to see what they were. The idea of turning over the whole kit and caboodle to the sheriff, admitting he might see evidence in the discards I didn't, dimmed my enthusiasm.

I put the cartons aside, discouraged. Sorting through both boxes had produced nothing that looked like evidence of a crime. The spurt of energy from the coffee had faded, and I dared not have another cup or I wouldn't get any rest before the next day's work. Yawning, gathering up the cat, I moseyed to bed. It was closing in on one o'clock in the morning. I'd sleep on it.

"Good night, Boots. Tomorrow's another day."

Chapter 4

I awoke with a start. Sunlight peered through the sides of the window coverings in the bedroom. *Could the white suit-style dress be Sarah's wedding dress?*

I leaped out of bed and hurried to the cartons. I dug out the 90's vintage dress, spread it on the sofa, and sifted through the one filled with papers and albums. I had only scanned the photos from the evening before. Now, I searched eagerly for the picture of Sarah Anderson with the man who might be her ex-husband. The ex was a tall man, somber-faced, with dark hair, who stood ramrod straight next to the woman in the pictures, the direct opposite of Fernando with his compact build, relaxed stance, and friendly smile.

One of the photos was a formal picture of Sarah and the ex. She'd been drop-dead gorgeous, in a graceful pose wearing the white suit dress. In heels, she was as tall as the man beside her. Her complexion was flawless, her hair was long and blonde, her cheeks round and full, and she had a twinkle in her clear, blue eyes. A true example of Scandinavian ancestry.

It might have been their wedding portrait, with Sarah holding a bouquet of roses and the couple gazing into the camera. She'd been ready to part with the memories of her earlier marriage just before she died. I stashed the picture in my purse. If nothing else, I wanted to show the photo to Myra and get her impression. I returned the dress to the carton.

I had a house to renovate, and it was nearly 9:00, a late start to the day's work. There was the old carpet pad waiting to be removed. After downing a peanut butter sandwich and banana, I dressed in a grungy gray sweatshirt and jeans. Grabbing my mug of Colombian brew, messenger bag, and leaving a treat for Boots, I dashed out.

Parking beside the dumpster, I was curious whether Fernando had disposed of any other cases. I peered inside the container. It looked untouched.

Unlocking the door and skipping up to the main level, I started my work for the day. Steadily, I tore up the carpet padding and removed staples, tossing the debris into trash bags. After about an hour of clearing the floor, my cell phone rang.

"Hello, Myra," I answered. "How's it going?"

"Not good. I'm letting the contractor duke it out with the framers." She sighed. "Did you find anything in the boxes?"

"Maybe. There were some nineties clothing and old pictures, receipts."

"Do you think the sheriff would be interested in the contents?"

"Don?" I groaned. "First, I'd have to explain what I was doing last night. That I was retrieving the containers that Fernando dumped. Then, he'd lecture me about snooping."

"You might have found them today? You didn't know where they came from." Her voice held a hint of mischief.

I snickered. "That's true. But I brought them home with me? Disturbing and possibly destroying evidence? Sarah's name is all over the receipts. He'd know they were from Fernando."

"Yes. And that's why you called him."

I played the devil's advocate. "It's a stretch. Why take them out? Why not call as soon as I found them?"

"He knows you *are* a bit of a snoop. He might be happy to get the cartons."

"Yeah. I don't know. He practically caught me in the act of salvaging them last night. He'd put it together."

"Yes. He might. But he may say nothing. You'd be doing him a favor."

"I doubt that's what he'd think." I winced. "More like, obstructing a police investigation."

"He can be a little by-the-book," she conceded. "You could return them to the dumpster?"

"Maybe." I considered the possibility. "No. I want to keep them and figure out if there's anything of interest to the police. If there is, I promise I'll fess up."

"All right. I've got to go. My contractor is on the second line."

I hung up and continued removing the padding and staples from the subfloor. *Too bad this isn't hardwood. I could sand and varnish. But carpet it is.* I finished taking out the last of the staples, left my handy mini crowbar on the kitchen counter, and swept up the remnants of the pad and carpet.

Taking a break, I took another gander at the bathroom mirror and vanity. The vanity was in good shape, but the cultured marble top was flaked and stained around the drain. A new top, faucet set, and mirror were in order. All projects I knew Wayne could do. But, if Wayne and Gillie got married or made a "commitment" in Vegas, would he want to work on renovations when he returned? They hadn't said where they planned to live after their ceremony, but surely, they'd want to set up residence together.

I decided to tackle the job. I had access to Wayne's tools in the garage at the townhouse, and I could frame out the mirror. I'd hire a plumber to do the rest of the work. With a plan in mind, I'd start by asking Fernando about the plumbing truck I'd seen earlier, I headed to his place.

"Hello, Katelyn," he said as he answered the door.

His smile warmed my heart and gave me pause.

"Hi, I hope you don't mind my dropping by…. "

"It is a pleasure." His chocolate brown eyes searched my face.

"I need a plumber to change out a sink and install faucets, and I saw a plumbing truck here a while back. Randy's Plumbing? How did you like him?"

"Yes. He was fine." Fernando shrugged. "Sarah liked him."

"What did she have done?" Plumbers are a dicey lot. In my experience, they charged a lot and were very independent.

"He installed a new garbage disposal."

"Okay." I waited for him to elaborate.

"It works." He shrugged.

"I might ask him for a bid. Was there anything you didn't like?" I frowned at his reluctance.

"No." He shook his head. "It was Sarah's choice. I'll get his number."

"That would be great." I dawdled on the stoop, waiting for his return, feeling conspicuous. The chatty neighbor present on the day of Sarah's removal walked past, the small white dog pulling her along. She waved. I smiled. For the life of me, I couldn't remember her name. My paranoia rose when she directed a second careful gaze, as if to verify I was the woman rehabbing the home next to her.

Yeah, lady. It's me. Get a cat. I did an eye-roll at her retreating back. Fernando came back with a card for Randy's Plumbing and handed it to me.

"Thank you."

"You are most welcome, Katelyn." His accent melodic. "If you wish to talk, it would be an honor to listen."

"Uh huh." I did a quick step towards the rehab. "Thanks, again." I muttered under my breath, "Do I look that miserable?" Shouldn't I be saying that to him? He was the one with the dead wife. I slunk back to the house, clutching Randy's info.

It didn't help that they were playing Lee Greenwood's "Somebody's Gonna Love You" on the radio for classic country day as I worked. A hard knock at the door interrupted my pity party, and I went to answer, hoping it wasn't the handsome Fernando.

"Hello, Katelyn." Don Williams stood on the front step; his keen cobalt blue eyes surveyed my attire. "How's the project going?"

"Take a look." I motioned for him to follow and we went up the steps to the kitchen. "It's fine. I just finished making a list for a plumbing estimate."

We stood in the small kitchen and he gazed at the bare floor in the living area. I was about halfway through removing the carpet pad. Tufts of fibers and foam were strewn about.

"Doesn't Wayne plumb?"

"Yep. He's in Vegas now, with Gillie."

"Wayne and Gillie are getting married?" His eyebrows rose.

"Commitment ceremony." At his puzzled expression, I added, "It's a long story."

He stared at me, abruptly asking, "So you have a plumber? Who?"

"I don't believe you've ever been this interested in who works on my renovations." I stared him down, perplexed.

"Sorry. It's a professional hazard. I ask a lot of questions."

"If you must know, I'm checking out a local plumber, Randy."

"Humm." His brows knitted; he lifted the pry bar by one end from the counter. "This is quite a tool. What's it for?"

"It's a molding bar, used to remove the trim and staples."

"Wicked looking thing." He examined it thoroughly. "Resembles a crowbar. How long have you had it?"

"Just bought it. At the home store." I saw the question in his expression and responded stiffly, "After Sarah's body was removed." He kept watching me. I threw up my hands. "Do you want the receipt, for cripe s' sake?"

"Hang on to it." In a softer tone, he said, "No need to get testy. I'm investigating a woman's death."

"Yeah, well. I don't like where you're going. I hadn't met Sarah and barely know Fernando. I wouldn't kill anyone!"

"I doubt you killed her. Did you lend out the tool? The neighbor says that you've been friendly with Garcia."

"Oh. Come. On! I just bought the thing! What do you mean by 'friendly'?" I gaped.

"Okay." He relaxed at my protest and said, "We had a report from a neighbor saying that they saw Fernando throw some items into your dumpster. I'd like to take a look."

"Knock yourself out." I felt myself turning a bright red. *Dang it!*

"Is there something you want to tell me?" His gaze was sharp, brows furrowed.

"I may have found a couple of cartons and taken them," I mumbled. Better I tell him than he finds out through yet another nosy neighbor.

"You did what!" His voice boomed.

I inhaled deeply. "He asked if he could dispose of two boxes in the bin. I said yes," I muttered. "Then I retrieved them and brought them home."

"That's what you were doing here last night?"

"Yes." I said reluctantly. Avoiding his gaze, I

swooped down and collected a piece of stray carpet pad from the kitchen floor.

"Did you consider he might be attempting to get rid of evidence?"

"Yes." I hesitated. "He said they were items his wife was planning to throw out, and I didn't see any harm in it."

"You believed him?" He was skeptical. "You were playing detective!"

"Maybe," I mumbled. I felt the sole of my shoe and discovered a staple wedged in the bottom. I slipped off the footwear and wedged the metal out, avoiding the sheriff's gaze.

"Katelyn, do not put yourself in the middle of a murder investigation!"

"Murder!"

"Yes. Murder. The medical examiner determined Sarah died from a blow to the back of the head. A blow too deep for her to have hit her head on the counter as previously thought. That's more than I should tell you. Now, stay out of it. I want to see the cartons."

"Don't you need a warrant?" I tried to stall.

"Not from him. He dumped them. Are you trying to impede the police investigation?"

"No." I gulped. He wasn't buying my delay tactic. Now that I knew Sarah had been murdered, I had to be sure the man in the picture I found was her ex. The photo burned a hole in my handbag. I hadn't had time to go through the receipts and papers either.

"I'll get the containers."

"I'll follow you and collect them." He stood firm, waiting for me.

"I'll meet you at my home," I said. *I could get a head start, and maybe do some digging.*

"I'll follow you," he repeated. His expression said he'd read my mind about searching the contents of the boxes.

"Okie, dokey." I gave up. I wouldn't get a chance to sort through them with the sheriff escorting me. I grabbed my bag, my face burning, and headed out to my trusty Ford.

The unmarked squad created a stir in the neighborhood when residents saw the interaction between the two of us. The neighbor returned from dog walking, stopped, and stared. Fernando lingered by his truck, and the occupants of cars on the scantily traveled street stared at our procession.

I gritted my teeth and ignored the stares.

Once home, I dashed to the entrance ahead of Don's swift gait. Unlocking the door, I threw it open, waving him ahead of my path. Boots made a beeline towards me, meowing, demanding treats. I picked him up and went to the kibble jar in the kitchen. Satisfied with a snack, he jumped down, meowed, and darted to the sofa out of the sheriff's tracks.

"They're over there." I pointed to the corner of the living room where I'd stacked the containers the night before. Don picked up one box. My dismay at being followed home by the sheriff's car and giving up the cases was momentarily diminished watching Don hoist the box with his muscular arms, broad shoulders, and firm butt.

Focus Katelyn!

"Coffee?" I asked.

"No time. Thank you for your cooperation." He left with one carton. Idly, I estimated how long it would take for him to go to his car, and considered how much I could remove from the remaining box before he returned.

"No problem." I decided against the last-minute

heist and filled a mug of coffee from the carafe and stuck the cup in the microwave. He was already suspicious of my motives.

He was back in a flash and lifted the last case. He paused. “We do need to talk.”

My stomach fluttered. “About what?” I sipped my coffee, feigning disinterest.

“Olivia.”

“Who’s Olivia?”

“My daughter.”

“You have a child?” I choked on the coffee and spit it out in the sink. Gasping, I swallowed, and wiped moisture from my eyes with the side of my hand.

“We’ll talk.” He nodded. With the carton secure, he left, closing the door with his foot.

Chapter 5

I returned to the renovation with my thoughts whirling. Don had told me he'd been engaged when he was a teenager. His fiancée had died in a tragic accident. Bottom line, they never married. When was this child born, and who was the mother? It was too confusing. I agreed wholeheartedly; we needed to talk. Part of me wondered why he wanted to talk to *me* about his daughter. Lately, we hadn't seen a lot of each other. Maybe he just wanted a woman's viewpoint?

But now, I had to get back on track with my project. With the old carpet removed, I needed to finish tearing out the pad. I was determined to frame out the mirror and get the plumber scheduled. I went to work on the remainder of the foam. After disposing of the remnants, I headed to the full bath, measured the glass, and calculated the amount of lumber to make a frame. I dialed the plumber Fernando and Sarah had used.

"Randy's Plumbing," a man answered.

Not sure that I'd heard correctly, I looked at the receiver, then asked, "Is this Randy?" This was a first for me—a plumber answering his telephone.

"Yes." His even tone was assured and calm. "Can I help you?"

"Hi, Randy. I'm replacing a sink top on a vanity and want a bid."

After asking a few questions, he gave an estimate. I thanked him and said I'd think about it. Truth was, the price was high. It was at the top of the average price range listed in my Google search for the work. I phoned three other plumbers from a home improvement referral website and left messages for quotes, as per usual. Then

I turned to the task of the mirror. Buying wood for the frame meant another trip to the store.

My cell phone rang, and I winced when I saw it was Don.

"Didn't I just see you?" It was a lame joke; I was in no mood.

"I called to apologize. I was a little rough on you." I steeled myself against his smooth explanation.

"Apology accepted," I said, curtly.

"Good." He sounded hesitant. "I want to explain."

"You don't need to explain," I sputtered and went off on a rant. "You think I murdered the woman across the street." *Okay, maybe I was exaggerating.* "You only now get around to telling me you have a daughter. You don't have to explain, anythi . . ."

"I'm sorry." He was quiet, and added, "I meant to tell you earlier. Olivia found me just before your water dump. We met at Ivan's and she wanted to show me photos of her mother and stepfather."

I was silent, absorbing his statement. I felt like a heel. My mind flashed to the two seated on the same side of the booth. No wonder he'd been distant. "I'm sorry."

He broke the mood, suggesting, "How about we go to Joseph's for dinner? We'll talk."

"When?" I relaxed; dinner out was cake. A meal at the fanciest restaurant in Hidden Falls, a half hour drive from Crocus Heights, was frosting on the cake. I practically drooled thinking about their food.

"Tonight?"

"Pick me up at 7.00." I hung up and motored to the home store for supplies and lumber, mulling over Randy's price for plumbing work. I'd budgeted for a vanity top for the bath and picked out a jazzy granite number and new faucets at the same time. While choosing boards for a suitable frame, I considered what

I'd wear that evening, and what in the world Don Williams would say about a child.

My mind on overdrive, I checked out. The store employee, a twenty-something bear of a man, picked up the granite sink top like it was a pizza and loaded it into the hatch of my economy ride. I angled the boards through the passenger's window, resting them on the carton that held the vanity. I missed Wayne and his work horse vehicle, Matilda. The roomy van carried tools, equipment, and lumber. There are jobs my trusty Festiva is less suited for. I could've borrowed the truck, but it was tricky to maneuver.

At home, I unloaded the boards in the garage, then headed in to find an appropriate outfit for the evening. That would prove to be the biggest challenge. After showering and doing my best with an assortment of hair products, I tried on three different outfits. Jeans and sweater, too casual. Dress slacks and sweater, better.

The slinky black cocktail dress that I'd worn on our date to the policeman's ball was the best look. Satisfied, I'd go full out hottie, more for my own bruised ego and to dispel any whisper of being a murder suspect. I couldn't believe the idea had even entered his mind. He must have been joking; he knew that I didn't have a motive, nor did I know Sarah. Still, it bugged me. I called Myra for moral support.

"Dinner with Don! Wonderful. He's such a nice man," she cooed. "What are you wearing?"

"It's just dinner. The little black dress."

"Perfect. But it is Joseph's. Fine dining. You never know?" Her voice was hopeful. Hope that one day I'd settle down with a good man. It was hard for me to believe Myra was twenty years my senior because she appeared much younger. Widowed from a long, happy marriage, her heart was in the right place. She wanted a blissful union for me and didn't hide her preference for

Don, and I tolerated her affinity for the sheriff.

"Myra, he said he has a daughter. He wants to talk."

"Sounds complicated," she mused. "Who's the mother? Where is she? You haven't seen each other for a few months."

"Six months."

"That's quite a while. Maybe he has something more permanent in mind? How do you feel about him?"

"I'm not sure." He'd called just often enough to remind me we were on each other's radar. My mind had relegated him to the "friend" category, as he suggested. Reluctantly, but there he was. Could I change that? Yeah, I could.

Myra chuckled.

Rap. Rap. Rap.

"He's here. I've got to go."

"Call me. Have fun!"

I flung open the door, paused, and stared. He wore blue jeans. A bomber jacket covered a plaid flannel shirt. His eyes lit up as he took in my form. "You look fabulous."

"Thanks. I'll change."

"No. Don't." He leaned over and kissed me on the forehead. "The dress is perfect."

"I thought we were going to Joseph's." I flushed at his compliment and the heat of his body close to mine.

"We are, but most guys wear jeans and flannel shirts everywhere."

"You're right. No one dresses up any more. I'll change." I stepped back, ready to bolt to my bedroom, and change into outfit number one.

"No. Please."

"I'll look out of place."

"Not to me." He grinned, the corners of his eyes crinkling, the deep blue numbing me.

"Fine." I reached for my staple, a black jacket, from

the closet along with my handbag. I'd cover up with the coat.

"No Buick?" I asked. I balked at the vintage Corvette in the parking lot. He'd gotten the car from his father and was attached to the beast. The vehicle brought out the race car driver in him and a panic attack in me. He drove a very solid silver Buick in the winter. Somewhat staid, but comfy.

"No. Just took the car out of storage." He smiled and gestured to the car.

Don drove the snazzy red Corvette, shifting like a driver at the Indianapolis 500 speedway. I hung on for dear life.

We arrived at Joseph's, and he threw the car into park with a flourish.

"You okay?" He turned towards me with a grin.

"Fine," I croaked. Chuckling, he got out and came around to the passenger's door to help me out. My knees wobbled as I stood up.

Inside, he slipped out of his jacket and handed it to the clerk. He gripped the shoulders of mine. I hesitated, and gave up the coat. Taking my elbow, we followed the nimble hostess. Winding between crowded tables, out of the corner of my eye, I saw a couple of men do a double take at my dress. A woman nudged her open-mouthed companion. Finally, we were seated and the wine was served. I gulped gratefully. I was annoyed with the people who turned and scanned my outfit, whispering. I shifted, fingered the shape of my glass, and gave the man at the next table a scowl. He turned back to his companion.

I ordered the walleye, and Don ordered a steak, rare. After the waitress left with our food orders, he cleared his throat. "Katelyn, the woman you saw me with is my daughter, Olivia. I know I've kept this close to my vest.

I want you to know the truth."

"All right." I swigged more wine and leaned back. "Tell me about it."

He settled in his chair and his eyes dimmed as he spoke, "I had an encounter which didn't lead to marriage. Felicity, her mother, never told me we had a child."

"You're kidding. Why not?" I frowned, watching his expression.

"It's no joke. Olivia's my child. She looks more like her mother." He sighed. "I was immature. I've changed, hopefully, for the better."

"Okay." I recalled the pert redhead he'd been with at Ivan's. I was embarrassed. I'd jumped to conclusions and dumped a glass of water in his lap. Why was I so sure he was on a date? Oh yeah. Eddy.

"I'm sorry I spilled water on you," I muttered. Knowing my apology was still lame, I studied my wineglass, and sent a scowl to a woman who stared at my dress.

"Apology accepted." He smiled. My heart fluttered with the warmth from his presence.

"I am sorry. But why didn't you tell me she was your daughter when I came to the station?" I asked.

"I wanted to get to know her better before I told anyone. Be sure she was, who she said she was."

"Uh huh." I watched his expression.

"I was young and foolish. Now, I'm trying to make amends, be a father." He was sheepish, embarrassed.

"All right." I wasn't sure how he'd make it up to Olivia.

"Thank you, Kate. I appreciate your support," he said soberly, and folded my hand in his. I froze and gave him a stare that likely resembled a deer caught in headlights. His grasp was very warm. He released my hand, and asked in a low voice, "So, how are you and

Eddy?"

I blinked. *He thinks Eddy is more than a friend. Well, he is, but not in that way.* "Eddy's Eddy. Lola, his ex-wife, wants to get back with him." I added, "Eddy and I are over as a couple."

"Uh huh." He coughed and shifted in his chair. "You're sure?"

"Yes." *What's up with that? Was that why he kept his distance? Eddy?*

Our dinners came, and he turned to his steak with gusto. I was hungry and dug into my fish. We satisfied our pangs of hunger and he continued, "Felicity married a man who raised Olivia as his own. From what I've heard from Olivia, he was an honorable man and a good parent to her. He loved Felicity. They decided to wait until Olivia was old enough to understand she had a biological father. Felicity's husband died, and she became ill. Cancer."

"That's rough," I nodded, sympathetic.

"Yes." He paused. The server came with coffee. He sipped his brew and coughed lightly. "Eventually, she told Olivia about me. My name was on the birth certificate, and Olivia found me after her mother passed."

He took another sip and gave a small smile. "She takes after me that way."

"The investigator part of you?"

"Yes. Her mother wanted to take the secret to her grave, but decided it was best Olivia know she had a biological father out there."

"You and Felicity never talked about marriage?" I hadn't had coffee yet and had enough wine to brave asking him.

Don coughed, and his color reddened. "It was a brief relationship after my fiancé died. I didn't know Felicity was pregnant." He was rueful. "I was immature and didn't treat her well, and ignored her calls, and she went away. Had I known...." His expression was pained as he fingered his silverware.

"But she married another man?" Having a child outside of marriage was a big taboo back in the day. Felicity had found a gem.

"Yes."

"That's very kind of her husband to raise Olivia as his own."

"It is, and I'll do my best to make it up to her and to the man who raised her."

My mind was on overload. Don's hand was very warm. His actions as a young man had been deplorable. I felt sorry for Felicity and viewed him with a jaundiced eye. Why had he been so irresponsible? It seemed implausible that Olivia wouldn't have seen her birth certificate before her mother died. I'd been a nosy teenager once.

"So, have you gone through the boxes?"

"I can't discuss an ongoing investigation."

"Oh, yeah. That." With an eye-roll, I took the last bit of food. "You can't tell me if there are any leads in Sarah's death?"

"Nope. Can't say."

I sat back and rested the rim of my wine glass against my lip, reflecting.

Now, I had two mysteries to solve. Who killed Sarah? Was Olivia really Don's child?

He left me at my door with a brief, warm kiss. Not too long, not too short. Just long enough to make me wonder what on earth was going on with him. Then, I got into jammies and powered up my computer. I was itching to research Olivia and Felicity, but with no last names it was a dead end.

I settled on Googling Randy's Plumbing for customer comments. Satisfied with several five-star reviews, I yawned and called it a night.

Tomorrow, I would frame out the bathroom mirror.

Chapter 6

I took the liberty of using Wayne's compound-miter saw. The power tool was set up at the back of his garage stall at the townhomes. There was just enough room to work behind his parked van. He'd given me the okay to use whatever tools I needed while he and Gillie vacationed in the marriage capital of the country. He may have had second thoughts if he'd known I'd get into the heavy power equipment.

I measured twice to be sure I had the correct lengths for the glass. My plan was simple. The mirror was fastened to the wall with clips; I'd chisel out the soft pine to accommodate the fasteners and glue the boards to the front. I'd seen the idea on a home improvement DIY website and thought it was slick. Wayne likely had a more professional method of framing mirrors.

My idea was to keep the plate glass mirror, disguise a bit of missing silver, and learn something new. Very green and creative. It was with a Darius Rucker tune running through my mind, "When Was the Last Time," that I started the project. I plugged in the saw, donned safety eyewear, and followed the 45-degree lines I'd drawn on the lumber. I'd seen Wayne operate the saw and was confident that I could manage the tool. I drew down on the lever.

The motor roared to life, and the jaws of the cutting blade looked treacherous. I kept my distance, lowered the handle, and the teeth of the blades shredded the wood, making the cuts. Satisfied, I unplugged the beast, cleaned the sawdust, collected the boards, and loaded them in the hatchback.

I made one last trip inside, gave a treat to a sulky

Boots, and checked my voicemail for any bidders on my plumbing job. One company had a trip fee to estimate the charge for changing out the vanity top and faucets. Another plumber flat out said they didn't work with cultured marble, the material on the original top. One didn't return my call. That left Randy.

I mulled over his bid while I drove to the Warbler house. The Festiva sagged, loaded with the weight of the granite and lumber. By the time I parked in the drive, I'd decided to hire Randy. His price was at the top, but he'd answered my call, didn't need a trip charge to quote the job, and had given his availability all in one call.

Plus, he was familiar with the neighborhood, having done plumbing for Fernando's deceased wife. He might have even seen something that would solve her murder. I phoned Randy and was in luck. He had an opening for that afternoon.

I hauled in the cut frame sections and taped them to the glass to check the fit. I stood back. The mitered corners didn't match. I marked the areas that had to be removed for the clips, thinking the corners would fit better once I removed them. Taking a chisel from my toolbox, I started gouging out the areas marked on the wood. It was slow going. Frustrated, I stowed the lumber in the living room and got ready for the plumber's appointment.

I watched for Randy's van and met him at the door. He was tall, with dark brown eyes, solidly built, and wore a ball cap. I guessed he was in his late twenties or early thirties. He was cool, efficient, and knowledgeable while he assessed the job.

"You have the top?"

"Yep, in the car." I walked him to the car's hatch, adding, "It's heavy."

Lifting the door, he pulled out the piece, his long

body faltering under the weight. "Granite, huh?"

"Yes." I nodded. "That's what people want."

He gritted his teeth and hefted the box, rested it on his shoulder, and trekked into the house. After placing the carton on the floor outside the bathroom, he raised his cap to scratch his bald spot. The lack of hair aged him, and mentally I added a few years.

Squatting, he took a cutter from his pocket and sliced the cardboard protecting the material. He leaned back on his heels and considered the new top. "The backsplash sits higher than what you have. I have to remove the mirror, and I don't hang mirrors." He squinted over his shoulder, looking for my reaction.

"Sure." Of course, a plumber plumbs. It's better to have the glass down while I futz with the frame, anyway.

He removed the mirror and propped it in the hall next to the bathroom. Carefully, he cut the old top from the wood vanity, pulled it off, and toted the marble to the entry for disposal. Next, he unwrapped the new piece and positioned the replacement top.

I stood by, watching his progress. "So, you've done plumbing for the neighbors across the street?"

"Uh huh." He peered my way. Randy wasn't much for small talk.

"Terrible about the woman who lived there," I added.

"Uh huh." He gave me a sideways look, as if to say 'back off, lady." I ignored it and kept chatting.

"I got your number from her husband, Fernando. He said his wife liked your work. That's why I called you."

"Uh huh."

"The police think the death was a homicide."

Randy stopped his work. "No kidding?" He hesitated. "I heard it was an accident. She fell and hit her head on the edge of the counter. She was disoriented, crawled to the bedroom, and died."

"She died in the bedroom?" That didn't jibe with Fernando's version. He'd said he found her in the kitchen.

"That's what I heard." He shrugged.

"Where did you hear that?" I asked, puzzled.

"I know the flooring contractors around here. Her husband had the carpet replaced. That's what Dewey said, anyway." He was brisk.

"Dewey?"

"He owns Fast Floors, on Main Street, in Crocus Heights."

"Good to know. I need new flooring."

"Yeah. Call Dewey. Tell him Randy sent you."

"I will."

Randy was under the sink, tightening the spigots. He threw aside his wrench, stretched long legs out from under the vanity, stood, and finished his installation.

"You've done a few plumbing jobs in the neighborhood. Is that how Sarah found you?" I tried to ask in a round-about way, but let's face it, the question was a bit nosy.

He straightened; his mouth puckered as he wiped the fixture clean. "She knew my dad, Randy, Sr." He was polite, but firm, as he efficiently sealed the sides of the backsplash. He tested the spigots, filling the sink with water, then draining the basin.

"Oh?"

"Done. I'll get your bill and put this in your dumpster." He gestured towards the marble piece he'd removed.

"Thanks. I'll get my card." He gathered his tools and headed to his truck. When he returned, he trucked the old top to the waiting dumpster. Shortly, he came back with a handwritten invoice. I handed him my charge card.

"There's a fee for a credit card—2-1/2%." Visibly annoyed, he lifted his cap, and rubbed the ridge on his forehead where the hat rested.

"Of course." I waited for my receipt. "Just curious, how did Sarah know your dad?" I shrugged.

"They were married." He was curt.

"Oh." I was struck mute. I wasn't nervy enough to ask when. She was with Fernando when she'd died. There must have been bad blood somewhere, so to speak. I hesitated, and blundered ahead, "She was your mother?" I frowned. Randy was tall enough, but the dark hair and the bald spot didn't fit with the picture of Sarah and the man in the discarded cartons. The fellow shown in the photo was a young, thin, dark-haired man. Sarah was a towhead. Then, I stared at him, fast-forward twenty-years; it could be Randy.

"No. She was just my dad's wife. She wasn't my mother. My mother's dead." He ripped off the paper and handed it to me. "Thank you for your business," he said coolly. He readjusted his cap and left.

"Uh huh." I shut my mouth and took my receipt and followed him to the exit.

As Randy drove away, I glanced out to see Fernando scowling, staring at the plumbing van's departure. Before I could wave, he disappeared into his house.

Oh, oh.

It was five o'clock. Time for a break and to compare notes with Myra. This was information overload. Don had a daughter he never knew about, and now the plumber had just revealed his father was married to the recently deceased Sarah. Was there any bitterness between Sarah and her ex—Randy's father—or her stepson, that led to her death? What in the world was going on with these people?

I studied the wood corners on the glass again, scowled at the mismatched mitered angles, and set the pieces aside.

"I'll try this project tomorrow."

Chapter 7

At home, I dialed Myra. "Do you have time for dinner?"

"Sure. Shall we meet at Ivan's? Six o'clock?"

"Sounds good."

I strolled into the restaurant with a minute to spare. Katarina led me to a booth, dropped a menu, and stalked off. Myra found me with Ivan's direction. The staffer circled back and slapped a menu in front of her, sniffed, and marched away.

"So, how's our favorite hostess?" Myra shrugged out of her coat, her eyes twinkling.

"The same," I said, snickering.

"Must be a shirt tail relative," she said; her expression muted. The cranky server rounded the corner to our booth, surprising us, and we ordered sheepishly, caught gossiping.

Myra turned her attention to me. "So, tell me what's happening? How did your date go?"

"I don't think I'd call it a date." I shrugged. I wasn't ready to consider Don's invitation to dine a date. Date implied relationship, and from what I could tell, we were still iffy. I'd never been very good at deciphering the male code.

"Uh huh. Trust me. Dinner at Joseph's in Hidden Falls is a date."

"Okay." I chewed my bottom lip. "I told you he has a daughter."

"Yes." She inhaled, sitting back. "Tell me everything."

"The girl's name is Olivia."

"Okay." Myra waited.

"Apparently, he had a brief relationship after his fiancé died. The woman, Felicity, married another man, who was a good dad to Olivia."

"Uh huh," she prompted.

"Felicity and her new husband decided not to tell the girl she had a bio father until she was older. She told Olivia about Don shortly before she died."

"Wow." She sighed and sipped her wine.

"Wow, is right." I winced, reflecting on the news. It sunk in as I filled her in.

"You seem suspicious?"

"Yes. Maybe I'm just a skeptic. But I was a curious teenager once, and I wonder why Olivia hadn't seen her birth certificate when she was growing up."

"Hmm." Myra rubbed her chin and leaned against the back of the booth. "Maybe she *had* seen it."

"You think Olivia knew about the birth record, but said nothing?"

"Or, she saw their marriage certificate, did the math, didn't understand, and figured it was better to keep mum?" she mused. "Hard to believe a teenager wouldn't say something if she'd seen documentation."

"This could be troubling for Olivia," I added, "They raised her to believe one man was her father, then she learns her bio father is someone else. I can understand why Felicity wouldn't have wanted to explain. Times were different."

"Definitely. But it sounds as if she had a happy childhood?"

"Yes. According to Don, her parents loved her and gave her a solid foundation."

"Now, they're gone, and she's finding her roots," Myra suggested.

"Yep." I gulped.

"How do you feel about being a stepmother?" Her

hazel eyes twinkled.

I groaned. "Let's not go there."

She relaxed and asked, "Okay. What happened with the boxes?"

"Don took them. He won't tell me anything about the case."

"Standard. Can't discuss an ongoing investigation. My brother pulls that all the time." She chuckled. Her brother was the chief of police for Crocus Heights. That connection had helped resolve the sensitive situation and any adverse publicity at the townhouse unit where my neighbor, Ariel Kominski, had been killed. They had renovated and kept the home off the market. It doesn't hurt to have friends in high places. Or friends with prominent relatives.

"Oh, but I have something!" I dug around in the massive messenger bag I'd adopted as a purse. "This!" I held up the photograph of Sarah Anderson and the man I believed to be her ex-husband.

"You kept this from the boxes Fernando disposed of?"

"Yep. I didn't have a lot of time to go through them before Don absconded with them."

She viewed the print. "Yes. It looks like the eighties or early nineties. Remember those shoulder pads?"

"Do I ever?" I chuckled.

"He doesn't know you have this?"

"Well. No. I took it before I knew he wanted the cartons. Besides, there's probably another copy in the containers." I was on the defensive. "When I retrieved the boxes, they were on my property, trash. Anyone could have taken them from the dumpster."

"True enough," she said, and offered, "If anyone else had removed them without your permission, it's trespassing."

"Yes. Legally, it's my trash in the roll-off. If

anybody wants old carpet, have at it." I smiled.

"Uh huh. She was beautiful," she commented, scrutinizing the picture. "Beauty can be a problem," she mused.

"Yeah. So, they say." I chuckled.

"Humm. They're both tall. He looks Swedish, Nordic?"

"Guess who he's related to?"

"Who?" She sniffed; her brows furrowed.

"Randy, my new plumber."

"You *have* been busy. How did you learn that?" She laid the photo on the table between us, perking up.

"I had Randy change out the sink top for the vanity at the rehab."

"How do you like him?" she asked, adding, "I can always use a good plumber."

"He was efficient. A little prickly," I said, remembering his annoyance that I'd used a credit card. "But he did the job. He answered his phone and was available."

"Good to know. A reputable plumber is hard to find."

"Uh huh. So, he's finishing up, and I ask about the woman across the street. How long he'd been doing plumbing in the hood, and all that. He told me his dad was married to Sarah."

"Sarah was his mom?"

"No. She definitely was not his mother. He said his dad and Sarah were married. He didn't say anything more. My impression was he wasn't a fan of the union." I reflected on what Fernando had revealed about him and Sarah enduring unhappy marriages.

She raised her brows, perplexed. "So he worked for his father's ex-wife?"

"Business is business. Doesn't mean you have to like your customers to do the job." I shrugged. "Maybe, she felt guilty about marrying his father? It must have ended badly."

Myra nodded. "Goodness. It's a small world. Did he say anything about her death?"

"He didn't know the medical examiner had ruled it a homicide."

"The police must have questioned him. They likely know he was a stepson. They may not have wanted to tip their hand that it was murder, until they have more evidence," she offered. "Both Randy and his father could be suspects."

"They could." I recalled the plumber's cool, efficient manner and how he'd tackled removing the vanity top. "Fernando could've told him, but why? Doesn't sound as if he'd have hired him for work. That was Sarah's thing."

"I leave bill!" Katarina swooped in and slapped a ticket on the table. A snort of laughter caught in my throat and I tried to squelch the giggle. Failing, I choked back laughter, fervently trying to stem the sound. Myra caught my case of the giggles. Finally, we sobered up, finished our food, and paid the tab.

I was driving home when I realized I hadn't asked Myra about the progress on the Hiptown house.

"Yowl!" Boots greeted me as I came through the door.

"Chow time, huh?" I fed him and stroked his fur. We settled in on the sofa.

The townhouses were far too quiet with Wayne and Gillie in Vegas and the unit Ariel had once lived in still vacant. The spare room, where Eddy would stay occasionally, echoed emptiness. The rehab was a solitary pursuit.

"How about joining me tomorrow, Boots?" I continued petting the cat.

He shot me a wary look, scurried away, and hopped

up to rest on the back of the couch.

"You're coming with me." My mind made up, I picked up the laptop, determined to find more information on Sarah and her union with Randy's dad. I retrieved his plumbing receipt from my bag and Googled Sarah Anderson Jackson, on the off chance she'd used Jackson along with her maiden name. Jackson was Randy's last name on the invoice. I added Arizona to the search line, and the article popped up, "Mesa Woman Fends off Cougar While Cooking on Backyard Grill."

The story went on, stating the mountain lions were losing their natural habitat and increasingly foraged for food in more settled areas of the state. The woman had faced the wildcat and had successfully staved off an attack. The article warned people to be on the lookout for wild animals that could be mistaken for a golden retriever.

"Wow. Sarah was lucky, or just very feisty." Boots licked his paws, and yawned.

"Okay. Let's call it a night." I powered down the computer and headed to bed.

Chapter 8

While loading an indignant Boots into my car the next morning, the phone rang. I secured the latch to the crate, shushed the cat, and snatched up the receiver, "Hello!"

"Hey, Kiddo!"

"Wayne! It's so good to hear from you!" The sound of his voice overwhelmed me with emotion. It hit home how much I missed my friend, neighbor, and handyman. "How's your vacation?"

"It's dang awesome. That's how!"

"Glad to hear it." I tried to sound happy for him. In the back of my mind, I was dreading another go at the mirror project from hell. "When do you think you and Gillie will be home?"

"Here's the deal. I thought we'd be back in a week, but we're having such a great time, gambling, seeing the shows, and the gosh darn wonderful weather, we're gonna stay a while longer. It's seventy degrees nearly every day! Plus, we scored a great deal on a condo."

"A condo?" I frowned.

"Yep. Rents from month to month. Hardly makes sense to stay in a room when we got all this space."

"So, it sounds as if you'll be away a month, or more?" I ventured, my stomach sinking.

"Yep. Couple of months. Figure we should be real snowbirds."

"Sure, Wayne. Do you want me to send you and Gillie's mail?"

"That'd be great." He read off an address. "Only letters. Don't need the junk mail." He laughed. I heard Gillie's high giggle in the background.

"Say 'hi' to Gillie for me. I don't blame you." Minnesota weather was a challenge. March was usually the snowiest month of the year. Mother Nature hadn't dumped any more of the white stuff, and the end of the month was in sight. But it could happen in April, May, or even June.

"How's the new rehab coming?"

"It's coming." My voice trailed off. "It'll get done."

"You got problems?" He heard the evasiveness in my tone.

"No, it's fine. I'm framing out the mirror. I used your compound miter saw to cut the boards. You said it was okay."

"Heck, yeah. Just be careful. That machine will mangle a finger if you ain't watching."

"Yeah. I noticed." Remembering the blade's teeth. "How's Gillie?"

"She's loving it! We're doing our Elvis commitment ceremony this weekend. It's gonna be a hoot!" He guffawed.

"That sounds like fun. I expect pictures and a full report when you get back."

"Ya got it!"

"Take care." I hung up and exhaled. Who was I to stand in the way of love?

"Dang it, Boots." I grabbed my bag and lifted the crate with the protesting cat. "Shush! You'll love my company!"

I pulled into the driveway of the rehab, determined to conquer the mirror project.

Up the six stairs to the main living level, I deposited my bag and unlatched the carrier. The cat darted out. Spooked, he investigated all the rooms up and down. While he wandered, I placed his bed in a corner of the living room, along with dishes for food and water.

Satisfied after roaming, he curled up snug as a bug.

"Just like home, huh, Boots?" I grinned at the cat.

Avoiding the sight of the glass and the framing boards, I trekked to the bathroom. The vanity looked spiffy. I viewed the rest of the room with a careful eye. The tub shower combination needed deep-cleaning, and a new toilet seat was in order. The fixtures were in good condition. A thorough cleaning and paint job might be the best place to use my energy that day. I got to work.

With a mixture of warm white vinegar and dishwashing soap, I sprayed the bath bay and let the solution soak. After several minutes, I started scrubbing. While I scoured, the doorbell rang.

"Dang!" I slipped off my rubber gloves and hurried to the door.

"Hello, Katelyn." It was Fernando. His eyes lit up and his face brightened.

"Hey." I nodded and brushed stray locks from my face.

"I would like to speak with you, if it is not too much trouble?" His presence was calming, his accent enchanting. "I do not wish to interrupt you." He glanced at the cleaning gloves in my hand. Boots was at my feet, and I stooped to pick him up.

"Sure. Come in."

We stood in the small foyer of the split entry, sharing a space of approximately six feet by six. I was very conscious of his body's warmth. He had a couple of inches on my five-and-a-half feet, with a compact build. Standing eye-to-eye, I couldn't believe this soft-spoken Latino man could have done anything to injure his wife. Boots protested my grasp, and he slipped from my arms to the floor.

"How can I help you?"

"I saw Randy's truck here yesterday, and I wanted to see how you liked his work." His earnest gaze caressed me.

"Yes. He replaced a vanity top." *Was he fishing about Randy?* I hesitated. "He was very professional. It looks great. Would you like to see it?"

"I would be pleased, if it is not too much trouble."

"Follow me." I headed to the bathroom, wondering if I should broach the subject of Randy's father.

"It is splendid." His face beamed, as he viewed the granite top. "He does excellent work."

I took a deep breath and dove in, "He said his father had been married to Sarah. Was that in Arizona?"

An expression of surprise flitted across his face. He recovered, saying, "That is correct. His dad was my wife's second husband." He chuckled. "I was number three." He smiled with even, white teeth. His eyes glowed.

"Oh? Three's the charm," I offered.

Fernando chuckled. "Yes, three is the charm. We were very happy. I am lost without my Sarah." Silence hung in the air and his soft gaze turned sad.

I coughed lightly, and looked away. He went on, "Randy is an unhappy man. He was angry that his father married Sarah so fast after his mother died. Yet, he was glad to get her work. Sarah felt guilty too. We met when she was married to Randy's father. She was very lonely."

"Sarah found you while she was still with Randy's dad?"

"It is true." He shrugged, and his gaze forgiving. "She was complicated."

"I guess." One had to be in awe of a woman who could pull that off. For me, it's one relationship at a time. Unlike Eddy, or it appeared, Sarah. Fernando seemed to justify or forgive Sarah's wandering. He didn't appear angry or jealous.

The doorbell chimed. I started, puzzled. "Who could

that be?" Fernando followed me to the exit.

"Hey, wifey!" Eddy pushed the screen door open and rested his long, lean frame against the side of the entry.

"Hi. What are you doing here.?"

"Yowl!" Boots made a break for the outside. Eddy tried to stop him by putting his foot between the doors. The cat darted under his foot. I leaped for the bundle of black and white fur and missed.

"Boots!" I yelled. Distracted by a squirrel, he ran for the brown, bushy-tailed rodent. As he closed in, I yelled louder, "Boots!"

"Boots!" Eddy called. Suddenly, there was a whoosh, and a huge owl swooped down, its claws extended. Its talons dug into the cat's body, and he screamed, "Ryowwl!" I waved my gloves at the bird, desperate to distract it from its prey.

"Go! Go away!" Frantically, I threw my gloves. One mitt hit the mark, and the bird released the cat. Boots hit the ground with a thud. His eyes were wide and frightened. He panted. Blood oozed from his coat, staining his fur.

"Eddy, why are you here, anyway?" I was angry and scared.

"I'm sorry, Kate."

"Sorry doesn't cut it. You can take us to the vet and pay the bill!"

"Sure, Kate. No problem. I'm sorry." His deep brown eyes, normally sparkling with mischief, looked hurt.

"Okay," I relented. "Get my handbag and a towel for Boots. Get his crate, too. I'll stay here." I was beside myself, stroking the cat, comforting him. He relaxed with my touch; his breathing evened out.

Eddy came back with the towel. "Here." I wrapped Boots and cradled him in my arms.

"What can I do?" Fernando appeared at my elbow.

"Would you lock up? The inside knob?" That would have to do. The dead bolt had a separate key, and I didn't want to take the time. "Eddy will get us to the veterinarian."

"Of course, Katelyn. Do not worry." Fernando headed to the front door.

I stood up with the swaddled cat, his body heavy. "Too many treats," I tried to joke while stemming his wounds with the towel.

"Let's go!" I motioned towards my Ford.

A police car cruised up slowly and stopped.

"What now?" I groaned. It was the sheriff. He hopped out of the squad and hustled to where I held the animal.

"Boots is wounded," he remarked, concerned.

"Yes. I have to get him to the vet. I can't talk."

"Hop in. I'll drive you." His solid presence commanding.

"What?" I asked, nonplussed.

"Get in. Remember, the squad has sirens and flashing lights?" He chuckled, his arm raised, and pointed to the back seat of the car. "You don't mind, do you, Eddy?"

Eddy was mute. I snatched up my purse and Don picked up the crate. I reiterated, "Eddy, you won't mind? The faster Boots gets help, the better."

"No. It's okay. You're right," he said, his voice subdued.

Don held the back door, and I eased into the seat beside the cat. He slid into the driver's side, and with one smooth movement pulled from the curb and started the emergency lights.

"You can do this?" I asked, stroking the cat. "Is this considered a police matter?"

He grinned. "I serve the public. It's not the usual

task, but I witnessed the whole thing. The bird attacked Boots. He's a great cat. Now, where's your vet?"

"His name is Dr. Katz, at the Animal Veterinary Clinic on Main Street."

"Katz?" He studied me in the rear-view mirror, laughter in his cobalt blues, his mouth twitching.

"Yes. Katz." I was in no mood for humor, even though the name was amusing in saner moments.

With that, he turned on the siren, and traffic cleared to let the vehicle pass. He drove the police car as if he were driving the Corvette.

I held Boots close as he gained speed. He whimpered, and I whispered, "It's okay. We're getting help." His body tensed, and he squirmed. We pulled up in front of the veterinarian's office, Don parked, and opened the back.

"Thank you. I can take it from here." I was grateful we'd arrived in such a short time.

"I'll walk you in."

"Okay."

He waited while I stepped out, my arms full with the frightened cat. He collected the crate.

I struggled to hold Boots while he twisted and yowled.

The young receptionist who sported black hair, thick black eyeliner, and a nose piercing watched. Her eyes widened and flickered over the cat cradled in my arms, with Don, in full uniform, escorting us.

"It's an emergency. I need to see Dr. Katz. My cat was mauled by an owl."

"I'll let him know." After taking my information and Boots' particulars, she said. "A tech will take you back." While we waited at the counter, I surveyed our surroundings. The reception room held two dogs and their owners. One dog, a sleepy older terrier, woke up long enough to give a short bark. An owner held a rambunctious puppy of undetermined breed on a leash while the owner shushed him.

A stocky, red-headed woman wearing a white lab coat came from the back that led to the examining area.

"Call me when you're done. I want to know how Boots comes out. If I'm not on a call, I can take you home."

"Thanks." I nodded, appreciative. *I think I'm in love.*

He pivoted, leaving. The view of his broad shoulders and muscled form which filled out his uniform momentarily distracted me. It was then; my cell phone emitted a muffled *FWEET FEW*! Don hesitated and stiffened. Puzzled, he scanned the people waiting in the reception area, shook his head, and strode out.

"Nice." The twenty-something receptionist smirked. She sported pale makeup and purple eyeshadow along with black hair and eyeliner. "Police escort." Grinning, she took the crate and handed it to the technician, who ushered us into a small examining room.

I must change that tone. My face hot, I dug out the phone, read the text. It was Eddy. "How's Boots?" I powered down and stuffed the cell back in my pocket.

The technician took the cat behind closed doors into another part of the clinic, leaving me to fret alone. After much pacing during a half hour wait, the doctor entered the tiny room with the cat. "Boots will be fine. The X-ray doesn't show any internal damage. I stitched him up and gave him pain medication. He needs to wear a collar to prevent him from licking his wound. Keep him quiet for the next few days. He had quite a scare." He was a friendly middle-aged man with a breezy manner and a sense of humor. He had brown hair and wore polo shirts and blue jeans, never a white coat, and spoke with a slight lisp.

"Thank you, doctor." I cuddled the cat. Now that he'd been medicated, he was calm.

"You said a bird attacked him?"

"Yes. There are great horned owls in the neighborhood. One attacked Boots."

"They'll rush a human if their young are vulnerable." He reached over and stroked the cat's head.

"I've heard that, too." Don had said the same, when news of Sarah Anderson's death broke.

"Dr. Katz, is it possible an owl could rush and attack a person, wounding them, like the bird did with Boots?"

"Anything is possible." He rubbed his chin, considering the idea. "They would be lucky to escape."

"Sort of like someone being mauled by a mountain lion?" I asked.

"It would be rare to see a mountain lion in Minnesota," he said.

"Of course. It was something I read. A mountain lion attacked a woman in Arizona, and she evaded the animal."

"It could happen with an owl. Not the norm, but a possibility." He breezed out, saying. "I want to see Boots in a week. Until then, watch him, keep the cone on, and carry on." He gave a brief salute.

I loaded the cat into his crate and grumbled as I paid the bill, cursing Eddy under my breath. He promised to pay, and I vowed I'd collect. Why did he come to the renovation, anyway?

It was about noon when I called Don for a ride. I was in luck, and he was on a lunch break. My stomach melted; he'd become my knight. I waited in the lobby and pondered the possibility that Sarah's death wasn't a murder. Could an angry owl have rushed the woman into the house where she'd collapsed?

Fernando said he came home and discovered her in the kitchen. Randy's version was they found her in the bedroom. Could both be true? Had she staggered into the kitchen, and disoriented, made her way to the bedroom? That would mean she left the bedroom and returned to the kitchen. I mulled over the scenario. It seemed unlikely that she'd go from kitchen to bedroom, then back to kitchen. Who was telling the truth about where Sarah was discovered?

Don arrived and again helped me into the back seat with the cat. I could get spoiled with this much attention. The goth-looking receptionist had slipped out for a cigarette and grinned, watching from the clinic's back entrance. She caught my eye and winked. I smiled and surveyed Boots. He was on his haunches, sleepy, his chin resting on the cone.

"Back to Warbler Street?" Don asked.

"Yep." My car was at the rehab. "Why were you in the hood this morning?"

"Patrolling the neighborhood. There was a report of another prowler."

"Oh?" I frowned.

"Yes. Probably kids. Lock the doors while you're working, be safe."

"Sure. I appreciate this."

"Glad to help."

"Do you think a great horned owl attacked Sarah?"

"What?" His brows raised, and he stared at me through the rear-view mirror.

I winced and repeated, "Maybe an owl attacked her? She was disoriented and staggered to the kitchen, hit her head, then continued to the bedroom?" Don's shoulders stiffened, and he peered at me with resignation.

"There must have been a trail of blood from the kitchen, if she crawled to the bedroom, and back?" I submitted.

"Katelyn," his voice heavy with forced patience. "We've been through this before. No snooping, and I cannot discuss an ongoing investigation."

"It was just an idea. I was curious, that's all."

He parked on the street in front of the rehab and bounded out.

"A possibility?" I exited the squad, leaned in to grab the crate, and twisted to face him.

"Can't say." He shut the door with more force than necessary. "No snooping, Katelyn!" He got in, shaking his head, and drove away.

"Harrumph." That hadn't solved the discrepancy between Fernando's and Randy's accounts. Randy had said Dewey told him Sarah had been found in the bedroom. How would Dewey know? Or was that important? Maybe it was a misunderstanding? What carpeting had Fernando replaced, and why?

I went indoors with the cat asleep inside the carrier. Boots was zonked from the effect of the drugs.

It was past lunchtime, and I was starving. I wrinkled my nose at the squished peanut butter sandwich I'd packed, and tossed the hastily made lunch in the garbage. Pizza sounded good. Strong coffee, even better. I didn't know why Eddy had stopped earlier. I wanted to give him the bill and tell him about Boots' condition. He'd texted, after all.

I retrieved the cat and left, locking the entry. The yellow cleaning gloves were scattered on the front lawn and I set the crate on the stoop to recover them. In my frenzied chase of the bird, I'd trampled the light snowpack. While I collected the gloves, I glanced to the planting area beneath the front window. The arborvitae bushes had been crushed; the bottom branches broken.

A metal object caught my attention; I moved in closer, pushed aside the bushes, and peered. It was a garden hand rake. Fresh shoots of crocuses were visible in the dirt beside the tool. Someone had planted bulbs last fall, anticipating spring flowers, and forgot the tool.

I plucked out the rake, unlocked the front door, and left it in the foyer.

Chapter 9

I blew into my townhouse loaded down with my bag and Boots' crate. The cat stirred. I spread an old towel on the sofa to protect the furniture, and set him down. After a halfhearted attempt to remove the cone, he curled up and fell asleep.

First order of business, I started a strong pot of Colombian coffee and ordered a Hawaiian pizza delivered, an addiction I'd tried to quit. Gluten, dairy, and carbs. A trifecta of all the evil food categories. While I waited for the food, I called Eddy.

"Hey, Katie," he crooned. "How's the kitty?"

"He's on meds now, asleep. Thanks to modern science and a big bill. Which is why I'm calling."

"You're calling about a bill?" he asked, and tried to kid, saying, "You know how to hurt a guy."

"Why were you at the house, anyway?" There was a silence from his end of the telephone and I braced myself for what would come. More often than not, silence with Eddy meant trouble.

"Lola wants to get hitched."

"Oh." My stomach churned. I gulped. "Do you want to marry Lola?" He'd suggested at one point that we remarry. I'd had to remind him we weren't the happiest wedded couple.

"The Bluebird house is too big for one person. It's nice having someone around."

I was quiet as I digested his logic. It didn't sound as if he were madly in love and couldn't live without her. It was practical.

"People get married for different reasons." I tried to sound diplomatic, but failed. "It sounds like a roommate." I was past Eddy taking up with Lola when we were married. Been there. Done that. But I still cared if he got into a bad situation. Especially since he was renting the house on Bluebird Street, I wanted whatever decision he made to be good for both of us. Our agreement, despite a few hiccups with his employment history, had worked. If he married her, would she want to live in a place that his first wife (yours truly) owned? If they remained roommates, she could move out on a dime. Wedded would be different.

"How does Lola like the house?"

"She likes it."

"Would she buy it with you?"

"No."

"Do you want to end the rent-to-own agreement?" With a sinking feeling, I thought, *I'll lose my tenant and have to get the property on the market again.* Exactly why I hadn't wanted to be a landlord. But, with the chaotic housing market and buyers in scarce supply, it'd been logical to rent it out.

"Not yet," Eddy said.

Great. The thing that had driven me nuts about him is that he could go with the flow and not make a decision. My disposition wouldn't allow for indecision with Eddy. Okay. Don was different, still unknown.

"Let me know ASAP."

"Thanks, Katie. I'll stop by with the rent check and pay the vet bill." It was the end of the month. April's rent check was a few days away. It could wait. "Really sorry about Boots, too."

I had a tiny twinge of guilt about insisting he pay for the veterinarian. After all, I was responsible for Boot's care, and it was an accident. He couldn't have known the cat was with me. It occurred to me that I was steamed about Lola moving in with Eddy at the Bluebird house, and this was payback. I mumbled,

"Thanks." Maybe, at some point, I could forgive myself for tolerating Eddy's antics, and forget the bill. Maybe.

The pizza arrived and I scarfed the warm soul food, fortifying myself with strong coffee. Being with Don that morning had reminded me of his daughter, Olivia. I was curious about Felicity, but still needed a married or maiden name to do a Google search for Olivia. I'd tuck that away for another time.

Fernando said he'd met Sarah in Arizona, when she was married to Randy's father. She was unhappy. He was unhappy. His visit to the rehab that morning puzzled me too. Had he come to warn me about Randy? To defend himself because he knew Randy was angry with him about Sarah leaving his father? Did Randy blame Fernando for causing his father's pain?

I had to get back to the property and get on with the renovation. Time was money, especially when it was possible Eddy might end our rental agreement.

I loaded a sleepy Boots back into his carrier, deciding he'd stay in his crate while I worked and could monitor him.

Back at the Warbler Street renovation, the glass was propped against the living room wall, taunting me, as I headed to the bathroom. I viewed my progress. In my haste to answer the door and rescue Boots from the owl, I'd left the mixture of vinegar and soap on the bathroom tile. The mix had dried to a blue goo. I sprayed water on the surface and started wiping the bath surround. The solution had done the trick, and a light scrubbing cleaned the tile until it shined. Pleased, I stood back to survey my progress. The sink and toilet fixtures would be next.

Rap, rap, rap! I answered the door to Fernando waiting on the stoop, surveying the roll-off dumpster.

"Hello?" I hesitated.

"Katelyn, I came to say I am sorry for your kitty's injuries and to ask if there is anything I may do to help you?" His eyes were soft and soulful. His dark hair stuck out from under a stocking cap. The wind was up, and the temperature was in the low 40s.

"Boots is recovering. He's asleep." Impulsively, I opened the door. "Do you want to see him?"

"I would like that very much. I love kitties." He entered, and his foot hit the small hand rake in the foyer. "So sorry. Are you gardening? It is a little early to garden."

"No. I found it in the planting bed out front." I gingerly reached for the garden claw, stepped to the main level, and placed it on the kitchen counter. He followed at my heels.

"Someone planted crocuses and must have forgotten it."

"Ah. I love the scent of the crocus flowers. They are the first blooms of spring."

"Yes. Some are quite fragrant. And, it has been a long winter and a slow spring," I commented.

"Too long," he agreed.

"Minnesota weather must be hard for someone from the West?"

"It is, as you say, challenging," he grinned. "I spend part of the winter in Arizona. I have family there."

"Good for you. It must be great getting out of this climate during the winter."

"Poor kitty," he cooed, spying the crate. He kneeled by the cage. "Can I pet him?" I unlatched the top. I had propped the mirror against the wall a few feet from the crate. Fernando's image was reflected in the glass as he patted the cat. I admired his gentle touch as he fussed.

"He'll mend. I'm grateful it wasn't worse. The owl could have killed him."

"Yes. That is true." He sat back on his heels, "But

we have much worse in the desert. Mountain lions have attacked humans. One got my Sarah. It is a miracle she wasn't killed."

"Really?" That confirmed my Google search that it was his wife, and Randy's stepmother, in the news article on the internet.

"Yes. It was before our union. It was why she left her husband for me. She was sure he had lured the animal into the yard." Union is a funny term. I put it down to his heritage.

"Really!" I watched his expression. He was pensive as he recounted Sarah's fears.

"Yes. She told me he left fresh meat behind cactus plants, beyond the patio area. About dusk, the lions hunt for prey. She went outside and surprised an animal feasting. The cougar attacked her. But my Sarah was fierce, and she fended off the animal with a long barbecue fork. She escaped and ran inside suffering only minor injuries."

"Amazing!"

"Yes. After that, she filed for divorce. She was certain her husband was behind the attack and wanted her dead."

"Why?" I was incredulous.

"His business was failing. He'd taken out large policies on both of them. She thought he wanted her life insurance money.

"What kind of business did he have?"

"He built residential homes."

"Okay." I nodded—the housing debacle.

"Yes. The market was tanking. People were defaulting on mortgages. The bank lent out too much money. It was how you say," he raised his arm, "very high?"

"Peak?" I asked.

"Yes, that is it, the peak of the housing crisis. The

economy was broken. Construction stopped, builders laid off workers, people couldn't afford to buy, stores went out of business. It was a terrible time for many people." He shook his head, recalling the years.

"Yes." I knew about that. "That's why I'm a home rehab specialist." I said with a wry smile. "How did you meet Sarah?"

"I am a painter. I can paint anything—interior, exterior, appliances, cars. You name it. Sarah's husband had hired me to paint their home, inside and out."

Fernando rose and wobbled; his foot lodged behind the mirror. He caught himself as if were an acrobat on a high wire. Attempting to regain his balance, he reached out and the glass bounced off the wall and landed face down. I heard the glass crack. Boots woke and yowled.

I dashed to help him, gripping his arm and steadying his back.

"Are you okay?" I held his elbow. Boots hissed from his cage. His body hunched and rounded, he backed to the farthest point of the carrier, resting on his hindquarters. He yowled again.

"Katelyn, I am so clumsy." He inhaled. "I got up too quickly and lost my balance. Please forgive me. I will pay for a new mirror." He spread his hands, contrite.

Numb, I looked at the remnants of the plate glass. "If I was superstitious, I'd say this means seven years of bad luck." I snapped out of it. "It's probably for the best."

"What do you mean?" He attempted to upright the glass. The cracked face gave way, and the shards of glass slid. I stepped in, "Leave it be. I'll get it," I said, and he left the broken glass face up.

"My handyman had a method for framing mirrors. It was slick. I was going to try another DIY method," I said, as I gestured to the lengths of framing material. "It wasn't going well." I shrugged. "So, a new mirror, it is."

"I will be happy to pay for the damage. Please, I will help you clean up this mess." His soft eyes pleaded. His head was down, his shoulders slumped.

"No. That's okay. It isn't your fault." I was already cheered because I wouldn't need to chisel out the wood for clips or get the mitered corners to match up. The project had become easier. I'd buy a mirror, already framed.

"I insist. I will purchase the mirror. Please allow me to do this," he implored.

"Are you sure? I don't blame you. I might have done the same."

"No, Katelyn. I insist." He was firm.

"All right. Thank you. I would appreciate it." If Fernando replaced the mirror, it would help with the bottom line of the renovation project.

"I will go now. I have done enough damage for you. Your kitty is angry, too."

Boots squirmed at the rear of his cage and pawed at the plastic cone. Fernando ambled to the exit and backed out. "I am so sorry."

"Uh huh." I nodded, wincing at the wreckage and the cat's protestations. I got out a liver treat, hid a pain pill in the snack and fed it to him. I stroked his body until he was calm enough to hunker down and close his eyes.

Now, to dispose of the destroyed mirror. I found a roll of masking tape in a bin of painting supplies in the Festiva. I put on gloves and taped over the large sections of glass to keep the pieces together. Carefully, I folded the mirror into smaller sections, then placed the sections into heavy duty garbage bags and trekked the bags to the dumpster. I swept the floor, pondering Fernando's visit.

He said he'd been a painter in Arizona. Did he do the same work now? He was too much of a klutz to be on a ladder. During his visit, he'd kicked the garden claw in the entry. Then he'd broken a mirror. All in the space of about a half hour. I hoped he was more coordinated on a work project.

"Boots, let's call it a day." I gathered my messenger bag and the crate with the sleeping cat and headed out. I glanced at the counter for the garden tool. It was gone. Puzzled, I put the carrier down to search for the hand rake and found it on the floor next to the dishwasher. I must have brushed it when I carried out the remnants of the glass. Relieved, I picked it up, noting a tinge of color, and placed it on the counter. In my haste to put the tool aside, I hadn't seen a residue of red clay dirt clinging to the tines.

I trekked to my car, trying not to stare at Fernando's home. In a sea of beige and gray houses common to the area, the deep sienna stood out. I'd considered it a happy, warm color when I met him. Now, it stood out like a sore thumb. His clumsiness left me uneasy about the soft-spoken man. Had breaking the glass been an accident? I shook it off. There were times I was a klutz, too. The exterior of his residence had a desert vibe reminiscent of his Arizona home turf, and you couldn't hold that against anyone. I shrugged, shook my head, and cheered by the idea of shopping for a mirror, motored home.

Chapter 10

Later that evening, my phone rang.

"Hey, Kiddo!" Wayne's voice warmed me.

"Hi! You must have ESP," I teased.

"Why? What's up?"

"I miss you. The bathroom mirror at the rehab broke. Like, into chunks. Now, I'm shopping for a replacement on the internet."

"Ya know that's seven years' bad luck?" he chuckled.

"I'm trying to keep an open mind. It happened for the better good. Framing out mirrors isn't my strong suit. Fernando, the neighbor who broke it, will pay for the replacement. It's all good." That was my rationalization, and I was sticking to it.

"Who's Fernando?"

"He's a neighbor." I gulped, and added, "whose wife died."

"Whaaaaaat?"

I hadn't wanted to burden him with the news that I was involved in another dead body mystery. After all, the handyman was on a well-deserved vacation with Gillie. The Warbler renovation wasn't haunted, like the Hiptown house, and I hadn't found a body, like in my first rehab on Bluebird Street.

"How'd she die?"

"The medical examiner ruled she died from blunt force trauma. The police are investigating the death as a murder."

"You okay working alone?" His voice was low and troubled.

"Of course, Wayne. I'm sorry. I didn't mean to

worry you! How's Vegas?"

"Gosh, me and Gillie are sure living it up." He laughed. "We got tickets to Wayne Newton tonight. It's gonna be a hoot!"

"That's terrific. Newton's performed for a long time?"

"Sixty years. He's Mr. Las Vegas!"

"You and Gillie have a wonderful time."

"But I don't wanna leave you in a bind?"

"Everything's fine. Believe me, I'm happier shopping for a framed mirror."

"Ya know, you gotta go with your strengths," he guffawed.

"Absolutely. You two have a wonderful time."

"Thanks, Kiddo. A couple of months will fly. Be back 'fore ya know it!"

"Enjoy! No worries."

I hung up with a sigh. Two months felt like an eternity. Little did he know, this project was a bigger challenge than I'd first thought. The plumber was creepy. There was a long list of projects. I hadn't finished deep cleaning the bathroom, and the kitchen needed a thorough scrubbing, too. I had to paint and have flooring installed in the bathroom, bedrooms, and living room. I still had to tackle the lower level family room, bedrooms, and bath.

The weather had been cool and rainy, not conducive to working outside, and the place needed curb appeal. The house had newer vinyl siding and the roof had been replaced, so that was a boon. It was good hearing from Wayne. I was happy he and Gillie were having fun, but I missed having the handyman's expertise. I called it a day, determined to get 'er done bright and early after a night's rest.

The next day, back at Warbler Street, I doubled

down on scrubbing the upstairs bath fixtures. Boots huddled in his carrier, wearing his plastic collar, and watched my progress with wary eyes when I stepped into his line of sight. Freshly brewed Colombian coffee gave off a deep aroma while I worked.

Rap, rap, rap! I dropped my sponge and went to the door.

"Good morning, Katelyn." The sheriff's deep voice cheered me, and his broad smile was contagious.

"Hello." He looked handsome and relaxed in his uniform, and before I could stop myself, I asked, "Do you want a cup of coffee? It's fresh."

"That sounds excellent." He grinned and followed me up the steps to the main level of the split entry. His presence took up all the oxygen in the kitchen, and he moved around to the side while I searched for a mug.

I found a cup left from the previous owner and washed and dried it, filling it with the brew.

"What brings you here?" My mind ran through potential scenarios. Dumpster violation? Neighbor complaints? Another dead body?

"Just a friendly visit. Wanted to see how the renovation was going."

"Oh." I relaxed. "Work is progressing nicely. Hunting for a bathroom mirror now." I caught myself before spilling the beans that Fernando had broken the glass.

"Uh huh. See you brought your helper?" He took the cup and gestured at Boots. "How's he doing?"

"He's doing well. Thank you again for taking us to the vet."

"No problem."

"Appreciate it."

"What are you doing with the kitchen?" He surveyed the area and spied the hand rake I'd left in the far corner of the counter. "What is this? A garden cultivator" He frowned, taking a step toward the tool.

"New paint and appliances. Refresh the cabinetry, mosaic tile for the backsplash." I'd been thinking about colors. "Oh, that? Someone must have been planting bulbs and forgot about it. I found it in the front bed."

He picked up the object and examined the tines, frowning. "This looks like blood."

My stomach sank. "I thought it was dirt. There's a lot of red clay in the soil around here."

"Where did you find it?" He went into interrogator mode while I defended myself.

"In the bed, under the picture window," I said with exaggerated patience.

"I want to take it, see what my lab people say. We have an unsolved murder, Katelyn," he chided.

"I thought the examiner said she died because of blunt force trauma. She was hit with a heavy object? Did she have other marks?"

"The death is still under investigation."

My gut churned. Someone may have been assaulted with the small rake. I didn't recall seeing anything about stabs in the news report about Sarah. But maybe the news wouldn't have included any details.

"Was there anything interesting in the boxes Fernando tossed?"

"Not finished going through them." He was brisk.

"Okay." Deflated, I had the feeling I'd hit a brick wall with the sheriff. "Sure. Take the tool. Glad to help."

"Investigating is my job. Nothing personal."

"Sure." Exhaling, I faced him, crossed my arms, and leaned back, my head resting against the upper cupboards.

"Do you want to meet Olivia?" He cleared his throat and averted his gaze from my shocked expression.

"Yes." I recovered, adding, "I'd love to."

"You can think about it." He squirmed and gulped his coffee.

"No, I want to." I won't lie. It crossed my mind I might check this girl out and see for myself if she was on the up and up.

"You seem surprised." He shrugged.

"I am." I raised my shoulders. "But I'd like to meet her."

"So, mull it over. Let me know." He studied the top of his shoe.

"No need to mull. Set it up." My brows rose, wondering if he was serious about my meeting Olivia.

"Okay." He grinned and set his mug down. "Thanks for the coffee." He grabbed the tool, carefully. "I'll take this."

I saw him to the door. Smiling, I observed his squared shoulders and jaunty walk to the police car. There's something about a man in uniform...

Then I came back to earth. There had to have been marks on Sarah that couldn't be attributed to a hit on the head. Maybe she was chased inside by someone wielding the garden claw. I shuddered and locked the door.

I wrapped up the bathroom that afternoon. It was therapeutic seeing the fixtures shine. The new granite top was stunning. I stepped back and considered whether I'd buy plate glass or a framed one with gray tones. Grays were all the rage, if it fit the space. I put that idea aside and stopped at the flooring store on the way home.

I pulled into the lot of Fast Floors a little after four o'clock that afternoon. Boots was grumpy at being crated while I did my errand. I gave the kitty a treat for his angst, with a warning: "This is a bribe, and you're getting fat." He settled down after snatching the tidbit.

I recalled Randy's statement that Dewey had installed flooring at Fernando's around the time of Sarah's death. He didn't say where the carpet had been installed. The mystery of where she died nagged at me. Had it been in the kitchen or the bedroom? His house had to have been cleared by the investigators, but if Fernando replaced bedroom carpeting, that could be suspicious. In any event, I needed flooring and Fast Floors was a good place to start.

I entered the store. The place was magical. I was used to buying carpet or vinyl at the big box stores where concrete and displays of fix-it products compete for buyers. Fast Floors was a serene oasis filled with racks of different colors and styles of carpet along with vinyl flooring. No huge rolls of carpet mounted on walls. The store was freshly vacuumed and immaculate. The displays were amazing. A nagging concern raised its head: they could be out of my price range.

Seated at a desk to my left, a teenager asked, "Can I help you?"

"Randy from Randy's Plumbing recommended Fast Floors. He said to ask for Dewey. I'm rehabbing a house and need carpeting."

"Dewey's my Dad. He's at a job today. My name is John. I can help you."

I studied the earnest young man, but refrained from asking his age. He stood up, and I considered the possibility he'd have a growth spurt. He was about five-feet tall, but neatly dressed, with dark hair. Acne splayed across his cheeks.

"Okay, John. I'm on a budget. The flooring is for a renovation."

"What price range were you thinking?"

I told him what I could spend, and he assessed the store displays. Taking a calculator from the desk, he led me to three different sections. "With a standard pad, any of these are an option."

"What's the difference between them?" I fingered the nap and studied the samples.

"Colors and thickness. The newer carpets have a better backing and resistance to pet stains and dirt." He split the carpet fibers apart and showed me.

"All right."

This kid was a professional and knew his stuff. "You can check out samples to see what looks best in the area."

"Perfect. I'll try these." I chose three pieces, and the youngster took my contact information and loaded the tiles into the hatch of my car. There was just enough space beside the carrier for John to stash the samples beside the crate, while the cat yowled and hissed.

"Poor kitty." John nodded. "Is he hurt?"

"He had an unfortunate encounter with an owl."

"Owls can be mean." He slammed the hatch.

"You sound as if you have experience?" I observed the young clerk, curious.

"Got them all over the woods in these parts. Had a pet rabbit once. Owl got it."

"I'm sorry."

"Yeah. Me too. Your cat was lucky."

"He was. When is your dad going to be back?"

"He's usually at the store late. He'll be here when you bring the samples back." He shrugged. "Bring the pieces back after three p.m,"

"How long can I keep them?"

"A week."

"Thanks, John." We shook on it and I headed home. I was impressed with John's flooring knowledge. He'd efficiently shown me what worked with my budget and educated me on the carpet. I was sold.

I dropped the samples at the renovation and kept a

look-out for Fernando. I hadn't seen him since he'd tripped over the glass. I was ready to give him a heads up about the price for replacing the mirror. His dusty red truck was nowhere to be seen. I shrugged it off and headed home. I wanted to do more comparison shopping, anyway.

At home, after I settled in on the sofa, with Boots fed, my tummy full, my computer up, and a glass of wine, I called Myra. "How's the Hiptown place coming?"

"Don't ask," she groaned.

"Oh, oh." I winced.

"Progress is very slow. The workers show up for a day or two, then they don't come back. They go to other jobs. At this rate, it'll be winter again before the inside is completed."

"Why don't they return to your site?"

"The economy is picking up. The contractor says he's taken on more projects, and his people want to go to those jobs, not mine." She sniffed.

"Bummer. At least the economy is better," I ventured.

"I suppose," she relented.

"Have you thought about calling Bernie back?" I asked.

"The ghostbuster? Why would I do that?"

"Maybe, there's some residue from the spirit leaving?"

"You mean like it didn't *want* to go?"

"Maybe the energy left from the vanished spirit is disturbing the workers?"

"Huh?"

"It's kind of like taking off a sticker, and there's that gummy stuff left? Could be the spirit is gone, but vibes left from its presence are there," I offered.

"Sounds farfetched."

"It's up to you. Think of it like Goo Gone for the paranormal." I had to smirk. It was the best comparison I could think of.

"Wouldn't the sage burning have done the cleansing?"

"Maybe it takes a deeper cleaning for some tragedies?" I submitted. "The contractor has performed, but with some drawbacks. Something isn't stopping the work, but stalling it?"

She was quiet, then said in a sober tone, "I'll think on it. I'll see what Bernie says."

"It couldn't hurt."

"How's the rehab coming?" she asked.

"It's slow. But I found carpet samples today. I had a thought about the murder, too."

"Any news?"

"Not really," I pondered. "Except Don was at the renovation today and left with a gardening tool."

"A tool?" she asked.

"Yes. It was a small garden claw. Whoever planted bulbs likely used it to rake the dirt. Crocuses are starting to poke through."

"Nice."

"It is," I conceded. "Don saw some red residue on the claws and thought it might be blood. I thought it was dried clay. We have an abundance of clay. Anyway, he has it now."

"Really?"

"Yes. He's having the lab analyze the stains."

"Okay?"

"So, something bugs me."

"What's that?"

"Randy told me Sarah was discovered in the bedroom. Fernando said she was found in the kitchen."

"Fernando should know."

"Randy says Fast Floors replaced carpeting at his house. By the way, if you're in the market for carpeting, this place is fab."

"Good to know. Go on."

"If Fernando replaced bedroom carpeting, that would be suspicious. If it was a living room rug, maybe not."

"Why not ask Fernando? Or Dewey?"

"I might."

"Okay?"

"I'd rather not."

"Why not?"

"I don't want to tip my hand. If she was found in the bedroom, and the carpet hasn't been replaced, maybe there's blood." I braced myself for Myra's comeback.

"How in the world would you find out if there's blood anywhere in his residence?" She was exasperated, reasoning, "Wouldn't the investigators have found it?"

"They could've missed it."

"I doubt that." Her voice was firm.

"Anyway, I have an idea."

"What?"

"It's better you don't know," I chuckled, and added, "Did you know you can buy luminol on the internet?"

"Don't tell me," she warned. "I don't want to be an accessory to anything illegal."

"What if I'm wrong? If I ask too many questions, that would make me look like a suspicious busybody, or flat out paranoid."

"True enough." She chuckled. "Good luck."

"Thanks, Myra. I needed to hear that." I disconnected and ordered luminol with an express delivery of two days.

Chapter 11

The next day while I was working at the rehab, Myra called, “I talked to Bernie.”

“What did he say?”

“He gave me a lecture on self-care. He said maybe I have negative energy that’s affecting the progress.”

“Really? That’s it?”

“Well, there *is* something else.”

“What?”

“He could do another sage burning and sprinkle sea salt around the foundation.”

“Sea salt?”

“And ring a bell.”

“A bell? Why?”

“It’s supposed to raise the vibrations for the entity and the salt absorbs the negative energy.”

“Are you going to do that?”

“I haven’t decided.” She was thoughtful.

“I’m in, if it will help with your construction. You know me, Myra. I’m always up to a new way of doing things.”

“I’ll set it up.” I heard her deep sigh.

“It couldn’t hurt,” I added, hearing her frustration.

“No. I don’t suppose it will. I’ll let you know.”

“Okay. At least you don’t have to dance,” I kidded.

“There is that.” She sounded happier.

“It’ll be fine. A little self-care couldn’t hurt. Maybe try a little meditation, a massage, soak in the tub, or get a manicure or pedicure.” I hung up and passed my reflection in the new bathroom mirror. *I could use a good hairstylist. In my dreams.*

Myra texted while I was cleaning at the rehab.

Can you meet me at Hiptown at 7 p.m. today? Bernie will be back.

Wouldn't miss it. I answered.

It was nearly dusk when I met Myra at the Hiptown house. She was perfectly groomed and her nails were freshly manicured. Her rosy complexion looked dewy. *She must have taken Bernie's advice on self-care. Good for her.* I smoothed my hair.

"Okay, so it isn't moving as fast as you like?" I asked. We stood in front of the Hiptown house waiting on Bernie. The imposing structure was framed out but was hollow and empty, awaiting work.

"No one has been here for a week," she said, exasperated.

"A week? That seems like a long wait in the building trade. They build at all times of the year. Summers are boom times. What does your contractor say?"

"Same problem with the workers. They show, then they don't."

"Okay?"

"The workers claim there are unsafe working conditions. Lumber moves from one location to another overnight. If they forget tools or their hard hats at the site, the items disappear. They hear noises."

"Huh." With eyebrows raised, I viewed Myra. "Could it be vandalism?" *Something is still here.*

Just then, Bernie sauntered up, his brown hair stuck out at odd angles. He wore tattered jeans and a tee shirt, and toted the backpack he'd had the first time we met. "Good evening!" he boomed, "You've had some setbacks with the construction?"

"Yes. The workers aren't showing up. My contractor swears his people are the most dependable in the area, but work stopped about a week ago," Myra said.

"I have just the ritual to get this job moving!" His tenor was high-pitched, and he grinned with gusto.

Diving into the pack, he brought out a small bell, sea salt, and sage. "This will get rid of any remaining bad vibes. Guaranteed."

"Guaranteed?" I asked. I was doubtful. Nothing was ever guaranteed.

"Yep. Let's get started; we want to do this at dusk. I'll ring the bell." He handed Myra the sage and a plate. "You take the salt," he proffered a small container. I lifted the cover. *Figures; I get to dispel the negative energy.* Myra lit the herb bundle.

"Now, I'll lead with the bell, we'll go clockwise. Myra, follow me with sage. Kate, sprinkle the sea salt as we circle the house. Myra, you ask the spirit to leave."

"Me?" She looked stricken.

"You own the house."

She blinked. "You're the medium."

"Just be respectful. Ask the entity to leave the premises," and he nodded, encouraging.

I bit back a snicker.

Bernie heard my muffled sound, and said, "You follow Myra with the sea salt. Let's get this done!" He rang the bell and made a path around the house. We followed in single file.

Myra said through gritted teeth, "If anyone is here, please leave!"

Bernie looked back at her. "That's the spirit…'er stuff."

I giggled and dropped a few grains of salt.

"Right." She stared at him. He turned back to the path and sounded the bell again. We continued the ritual around the dwelling and then around the perimeter of the lot.

Bernie halted when the sage bundle and salt ran out. By this time, darkness had fallen and streetlamps threw out dim light. He plucked out a cell phone and said,

“Got to go. I have a fare a few blocks over. Ladies, we did it!” He collected the empty containers from Myra and me and stashed them along with the bell in his pack.

“Fare?” Myra asked.

“Ladies, I’m full service. Ghostbuster, Lyft driver, and marriage officiator,” he intoned. “I must go.” He kneeled to zip his pack, ran his fingers through his hair, and stood. He sniffed the air. “This space is clean!” And he sauntered off into the night. We watched until he disappeared from view.

“He’s something else,” I said.

“He is. But I don’t care if he levitates or grows fangs if what he did gets this house back on track.”

“I agree.” Then I paused, considering her statement. “That would freak me out.”

“Levitation or fangs?” she asked, with a twinge of laughter.

“Both!”

After watching Fernando’s comings and goings for some time, it appeared his habit was to come home for lunch most days. With the luminol on order, I made my move the following day. I stashed a baggie in my jeans pocket along with a small scissors. I gave Boots a treat, and a thumbs up before leaving for Fernando’s place. I’d seen him go inside, and I wanted to catch him before he started eating.

“Katelyn, what a surprise. Please come in.” He greeted me with a wide smile, and his eyes softly glowed.

Said the spider to the fly.

“Thanks. I hate to bother you, but I have the information for a replacement mirror,” and offered the data sheet.

“Of course. Let me get my checkbook. Have a seat,”

he urged, pointing to the kitchen.

"May I use your restroom? I should have gone before I came." I shrugged and chuckled. "Small bladder." He stood on the threshold between the kitchen and the living room. His living area was compact, with a brown leather sofa and matching chair opposite a large television. The kitchen had a woman's touch with a wallpaper border and a crisp white curtain.

"Be my guest," and he gestured toward the room.

I entered the bathroom and closed the door. Inside, I spied another door. Puzzled, I cracked it open and gave a silent cheer. *Hog dog!* It was an adjoining entry to the master bedroom. I scanned the bedroom, looking for any evidence that Sarah died there, while keeping an ear open for footfalls through the home.

The possibility that Fernando kept his checkbook in one of the side tables crossed my mind. I paused and listened. His footsteps sounded from the living room of the small ranch-style house. I hurried to the bed, holding my breath while searching around and beneath the area. I figured it was the most logical place for his wife to have expired and lost blood.

Beside a side table, under the bed, I spotted a splotch of red on the tan carpet. I exhaled. This must have been Sarah's side of the bed.

"Are you okay?" He was outside the bathroom, just a couple of feet from the bedroom door. I prayed he wouldn't enter and catch me searching the area. Snipping a few fibers from the stained area, I jammed the threads into the baggie, and tiptoed to the restroom.

"I'm okay. My breakfast came up," I said, and I coughed. "I'll just be a second." After flushing the toilet, I started the water spigots.

"I have Pepto Bismol. It's in the medicine cabinet," he called over the sound of the water.

"Thanks. I'll do that." I opened the cupboard,

scanned the shelves, and grabbed the bottle of stomach aide. On the shelves behind the Pepto was a prescription bottle. The label identified the script for Sarah Anderson.

"Did you find it?" Fernando was outside the door.

"Yes." I coughed. "I think I have another spell coming on. It'll be a minute." I quickly opened the prescription container, slipped out a pill, and hid the tablet in my jeans pocket. I'd check it out later. My heart raced. Flushing the toilet again, I grabbed the container of stomach aide. Wiping my forehead and feigning nausea, I opened the door. He stood, waiting.

"Are you okay?" he asked. His gaze was hypnotic and full of empathy.

"Yes." I wiped my forehead. "I'm so sorry. It must have been a bad egg."

"Please take some medicine," he urged. "I'll get you water." I followed him to the kitchen.

"Yes. You're right. It couldn't hurt." I doubted that a little Pepto would do any harm, and it would discourage any suspicion on his part.

Seated at the kitchen table, he brought a glass of water and I chucked down a dose of Pepto in the plastic cup.

"Good. You'll feel better, soon." He sat across from me and wrote out a check. "This will cover the mirror. Again, I'm sorry for my clumsiness."

"Thank you. I'll let you have your lunch." I got up, feeling a flush of color across my cheeks.

"Yes. I must get back to work. I'm painting a big house today. My time is almost over." He led me to the exit.

"I'm sorry if I delayed your break."

"It's no problem. Stop by, anytime." His voice was low and soft. The flush traveled from my neck through my body, reaching my toes. If I didn't know better, I would've thought he was flirting with me.

"He *was* flirting with you!" Myra said and laughed. I called her the minute I was safely back inside the Warbler rehab, flustered by my encounter with Fernando.

"Stop. I feel bad enough I raided his toiletries and clipped the carpet."

"He has a thing for you. Just saying. He's available." She giggled.

"Oh, boy," I groaned.

"What are you going to do with the pill?"

"Identify it."

"How?"

"Mr. Google. It has markings. It was fluxoid-something?"

"Mr. Google knows all." She sighed.

"Yep." I stood at the front window and watched as Fernando backed out of his drive. "He's gone. I'll call you later. I'm going home." Sleuthing made me hungry and I was curious about my loot from his place.

I stopped at the mailboxes and picked up the day's mail. Wayne and Gillie's stack of mail was growing. I collected the pile and boxed it up to send to the rental condo in Nevada. I hoped they wouldn't be gone any longer than the two months he'd said. I missed him. The handyman and neighbor was good company and knew how to do anything.

I made peanut butter toast for lunch, sat down at the table, and powered up my laptop. I entered what I remembered from the bottle and Google filled in the rest. Fluoxetine. Generic Prozac.

WebMD provided the specifics for the drug and the common side effects. Dizziness was second on the list of problems. That fit with the gossip from the chatty neighbor that Sarah had dizzy spells. It might have been a result of the drug she was taking for depression. Or was it something else? I'd grabbed the only item I'd seen with Sarah's name on it. The rest looked like aspirin, ibuprofen, Benadryl, and the like. For that matter, if she took Benadryl along with an antidepressant, the combination could easily mean vertigo and sleepiness.

Satisfied I'd found the identity of the drug, I now had to wait. Delivery for the luminol was still a day off. The lull gave me time to get paint and supplies for the rehab. I could send off Wayne's and Gillie's mail, deposit Fernando's check, go to the store, purchase the mirror and materials. My afternoon planned, I headed out. I left Boots in the townhouse. He was happy to be at home, cleaning his paws, and lounging on the couch.

I'd need to compare the paint swatches with the carpet samples, so I took several brochures of colors. Later, I'd look at them in the house. I picked up a gallon of cool, creamy white paint for the main bath and chose a classic gray framed glass. It was more than I cared to spend, but Fernando had paid for the piece and it would dress up the bathroom. A store clerk loaded the new purchase.

With no room to spare and the hatch ajar, the crew member secured the box with rope and I drove to the renovation, wondering how I'd get it in. I passed Randy's plumbing truck pulling out of the driveway of the corner house on Warbler Street.

"Never good, a plumber in the neighborhood," I muttered. Fernando's red truck was parked in his drive. *Home already?*

I went to the back of my Ford, cut the ties that held the boxed mirror and studied the problem.

"You are feeling better, Katelyn?" I jumped. I was so engrossed in considering how to move the item inside, I hadn't heard Fernando walk up.

"Yes. Thank you for asking. You had a short day?" There was that dreaded flush on my face again.

"Yes." He motioned toward the box. "You have a problem?"

"I do." I nodded. "This is the mirror I bought for the bath."

"You will need help?" he asked, observing the bulky box.

"Yes." I reached in and tugged a corner of the carton.

"No problem. I will help. I will take one end."

"Great!" Hesitating a moment, the reason for replacing the plate glass flashing through my mind, I guided the box to his outstretched hands and he grabbed the other end. Moving in tandem, we hoisted the box onto the stoop where we let it sit, and I unlocked the door.

"Where do you wish to put it?" He carried his end of the box effortlessly, and I was grateful to have his help.

"Let's lean it against the wall outside of the bathroom." The deed accomplished, he straightened.

"You are set. I will go."

"Thank you." I avoided his gaze, feeling guilty about my earlier visit. I followed him out to my car.

"*Adiós*!" he grinned, waived, and headed to his residence.

"*Adiós*." I grabbed my bag, to go-cup, and purchases from the car, proceeding inside.

Trekking upstairs, pleased to have the mirror moved without a lot of grief, I carried my travel mug to the coffeepot intending to fill up on strong java. I dropped it and screamed. Beside the Mr. Coffee lay a huge dead rat.

After I stopped shrieking, I dialed the sheriff.

Chapter 12

"Could be a prank?" Don said as he viewed the rat. The corners of his eyes crinkled as he smiled. "Eddy?"

"Yeah, Eddy might think it was funny, but he knows better." He knew I had a low tolerance for mice and creepy crawlies. Even at our worst, he'd never threaten me with rodents or snakes. This wasn't normal vermin like a small field mouse; it was a dead rat from god knows where. Besides, this rodent was displayed in a men's size nine shoe box. "Thugs send this kind of thing to warn people," I retorted.

"Have you been watching those crime shows again?" His eyebrow arched, he studied me.

"It's been on the news, for cripes' sake!" I glared at him.

"Now calm down. Let's just try to figure this out. It's a common brown Norway rodent," he observed.

"I don't give a fig about its ancestry! I want to know who put it here and why!"

"Do you have any reason to believe someone would threaten you?"

"No." I shook my head and my bushy, dark locks flew. I must have been a sight, because a brief smile flickered across his face.

"Are any of your neighbors upset with you redoing the house? Any complaints about mess or noise?"

"I don't think so. I've met one neighbor, a chatty woman, besides Fernando."

"Uh huh." He pressed his lips together and examined the dead animal. He inspected the area around the rat, rubbing his temple, thoughtful.

"But it couldn't be him. He just paid for the mirror

he broke. It was an accident," I said in a rush, protesting. Oops, I hadn't wanted to tell him that Fernando had broken the plate glass.

He shot me a stare, digesting that nugget of information. "So, he's been here?"

"Yes." I replied glumly. After the kindness the neighbor had shown by replacing the mirror, and helping to tote it inside, I felt like a traitor.

He ignored my sullen admission and asked, "Who's the lady you're talking about?"

"She lives next door and is talkative, but I don't remember her name." She'd been one of the neighbors that congregated on the front lawn, watching investigators remove Sarah's body.

"Humm. I'll take a report and look around. In the meantime, I suggest you call an exterminator. It might be a neighborly way of letting you know you have a problem. People can be strange."

"All right." I'd add that to the list of charges that the renovation was racking up. Great. Possibly I have passive aggressive neighbors, or rats. Neither were good selling points.

"Is anything missing?"

"I don't think so." I'd called in a panic and ran outside. On my way, a cursory glance at the main floor revealed everything looked as I'd left it. There wasn't much to see downstairs. Don had arrived within minutes, and his presence was a breath of fresh air while he poked around. He was an oasis of calm and sensibility, developed from years of seeing people at the worst times. "I'll look again."

"I'll check doors and windows downstairs." He headed to the garden level.

He yelled a few minutes later while I walked through the upstairs bedrooms, bath, and living area, "I found where they got in!"

"Where?"

"The garage access door isn't locked!"

I couldn't remember the last time I'd used the back entry to the garage. Sometimes I entered through the lower level from the attached garage. Tramping through the narrow passage from the basement, and up two sets of short stairs to the main level, was troublesome. Lately, I'd come in through the front entry with supplies. It was fewer steps. And it was too early to tackle the backyard landscaping, when I'd need access through the back door for tools stored in the garage.

"Okay." I shrugged. I waited while he tramped upstairs.

"I'll make a note of the door and take the rat," he advised. He slipped on disposable gloves and gingerly placed the box with the dead animal into a plastic bag.

"Please!" My stomach roiled, and I shuddered, watching his movements. "Yuck."

"I'll get back to you if I find something. Lock all the doors while you're here, and when you leave."

I bristled at his tone. "I haven't used that exit in ages. Anyone could have entered the garage and unlocked it while I was working."

"Keep the main door to the garage shut." He countered in a no-nonsense tone. His expression was somber, and I backed off.

"Yes." I sighed. "I will." He was right. I hadn't locked every door every moment. I had to be more careful. The dumpster in the driveway had become a fixture. It would be easy for an intruder to duck beside the container and enter through the open garage undetected. Even a kid who wanted to play a prank.

I'd keep the dumpster until I finished with demolition of the carpet on both levels and disposed of any items. One floor at a time.

I ushered the sheriff to the exit.

"Thanks, Don." I locked up after he left. Then I checked each window and exit, verifying everything was secure. When I was satisfied, I called Myra.

"Hi, Myra. Got a question."

"Yes?"

"What exterminator did you use for your raccoon problem?"

There was a pause on the other end. "It was Exterminators R Us, and I won't ask." Her tone was dry. Myra often had problems with creatures, like ducks and geese invading her lakeside home, which exasperated her. Recently, it had been raccoons who'd gained access to her attic.

"Thanks, Myra. I'll fill you in later."

"No problem."

I called the exterminator, reminding myself that even homes in the best part of town had pest issues. The nice lady said they'd have a pest control expert out first thing in the morning.

Then I took out ammonia, bleach, and vinegar, slipped on cleaning gloves, and scrubbed every inch of the kitchen. I considered the coffeemaker, winced, and tossed the item into the garbage. It would only remind me of the deceased rodent.

After I finished disinfecting the kitchen, I used the box cutter on the cardboard that held the new mirror.

"This is perfect." Satisfied, I stood back, admiring the piece, and had another revelation. "Yep. I need a sage burning."

Reinvigorated, I spent the rest of the day comparing paint chips to the carpet samples. I marked the paint color that worked the best with the carpet I chose and headed back to Fast Floors. It was after three p.m., the time John said Dewey would be in.

I entered the store, my arms loaded with carpet tiles. I dropped them on an empty table, and asked the silver-haired woman who'd greeted me, "Is Dewey here?"

"He's on a job. What can I help you with?"

"Nothing right now. I'm returning carpet samples." I left the pieces and joined her at the desk. "I like this one." The woman marked the information on a card. "Call when you're ready for measuring, Dewey is usually here. It's been a busy day."

"I will." I headed out. *Lady, you have no idea the kind of day I've had.*

Visions of a hot shower, dinner, and a large glass of wine played across my mind as I drove home, exhausted.

Chapter 13

I popped out of the shower, slipped into sweats, and wrapped my hair in a towel. On my way to the kitchen, I jumped when I spotted Eddy lounging on the sofa.

"Yo, wifey!" He held a beer in one hand, waved a check in the other, and grinned.

"What are you doing here? You're supposed to knock!"

"I did. No answer. I let myself in."

"Give me your key!" I held out my hand.

"I didn't think you'd mind." He dug in his pocket for the emergency key I'd given him. He sounded hurt, and while he searched, I changed my mind.

"Never mind." I might want him to enter the house at some point. I wouldn't want him to break in. And I was almost happy to see him. Almost.

"What's this?" I snatched the check from his hand.

"The Bluebird rent and money to cover the vet bill."

"Good." I pocketed the check.

"What size shoe do you wear, Eddy?" My eyes narrowed, checking out his athletic shoes.

"Twelve. Why?"

I relaxed. Eddy hadn't put the rat in my rehab as a prank. He wouldn't go out of his way to find a box smaller than his shoe size.

"Someone left a rat in a shoebox at the renovation today. On the kitchen counter."

"No kidding! Isn't that what mobsters do?"

"Yeah. So, I've heard." I sighed.

"So, what now? What can you do about it?" He shrugged and sipped his beer.

"I called the sheriff, and he made a report. I have an

exterminator coming in the morning."

"Oh, Katie. I'm sorry." He sounded sympathetic, but from the gleam in his eyes and the way his lashes fluttered, I could see he thought the vermin was humorous.

"It's not funny."

"How about I order a pizza? Your favorite?"

I brightened at the thought of hot food. A hot Hawaiian pizza, delivered.

"What about Lola?"

"Lola and I are on a break." He studied his beer bottle and yawned.

"Break? I thought you were talking marriage?"

"It's complicated."

"I've heard that before. Pizza it is." I dialed the local delivery franchise and ordered a large pie. Tomorrow would be a big day. Dr. Katz would take out Boots' stitches. I wanted to hang the new mirror in the rehab. It was a good night to celebrate, even with the specter of a dead rodent.

"Hey, can I bunk in your spare room tonight?" After gorging ourselves on pizza, a beer for Eddy, and wine for me, he had enough of a leer that I hesitated. "No hanky panky," he added.

"It's that bad? You don't want to go home?"

If Eddy heard, he didn't respond. Instead, he took a gulp of beer and looked away.

"Okay. But I have a favor to ask."

"Name it." He grinned.

"Would you help me hang the new mirror at the rehab?"

"When?"

"Tomorrow, after work?"

"You got it, babe." "Babe" wasn't much better than "Wifey," but I let it go.

When the telephone rang the next morning, I heard Eddy answer. I choked on toothpaste, unable to stop him, and gritted my teeth.

"It's Myra!" he yelled. I finished brushing at warp speed, then I heard a knock at the door. "Hey, wifey. It's the sheriff." I did an eye-roll and ran a comb through my hair.

I gave Don a short wave and took Myra's call. Eddy languished by the coffeepot, a mug of java in hand. The sheriff stood stiffly in the entry, waiting, his expression blank.

"Hello, Myra?"

"I won't keep you. I was curious whether you reached the exterminator. You're busy? Was that Eddy that answered?"

"Yes, yes, and yes."

"Is that the sheriff I hear?" Eddy had poured Don a mug of coffee and asked about the red Corvette he drove spring and summer.

"That would be another yes."

"Call me, later. I want to know everything," she said in a low voice.

"I will." I hung up. Don had moved from the foyer and kibitzed with Eddy in the kitchen.

"So, you're driving the Corvette full time now?" Eddy asked.

"Yes. I take it out of storage as soon as I can. Great car. Don't make them like that anymore."

"Awesome!"

"We'll get in another ride," he promised. Once, he'd taken Eddy home after he'd gushed over the snazzy car.

Great, male bonding.

"I'd like that! Katie says a rat was left at the house yesterday? Any leads?"

"Eddy, don't you need to leave? For work? Now?" I

asked.

"No word on the vermin yet. The lab's checking it out," Don said, and cleared his throat, viewing Eddy, his brows knitted.

"I'll go." Eddy put down his mug and addressed me. "Good pizza, good night." With a wink, he grabbed his jacket and departed with a broad grin.

"That Eddy's a friendly guy." I detected a note of snark.

"He is that," I nodded, hiding a small grin. I couldn't explain Eddy, and the mischievous part of me wanted to leave Don wondering. "What brings you here?"

"Isn't today the day Boots gets his stitches out?"

"Yes?" Then it registered that he was out of uniform, wearing his bomber jacket, jeans, and a blue shirt.

"Do you want company? I'm off." His face took on a warm glow. His hair was neatly brushed.

"I would love company." I grabbed my jacket and bag, and gathered Boots into his crate; the cat yowled, protesting. I shrugged off a guilty twinge about not explaining Eddy. After all, I was single.

I halted and winced at Don's snazzy red auto parked in front of the building.

"Let's take my car," I said. I loaded the crate into the Ford's hatch, and Don slid into the passenger's seat.

Dr. Katz examined the sulky cat, removed his stitches, and pronounced him in good shape.

"Thanks for coming," I said to Don afterwards. "I'll drive you to your car."

We arrived at the townhouse. "Thanks again for keeping me company." I killed the engine, waiting for him to leave. Instead, he reached over and placed his hand over mine and I felt a tingle.

"Would you have time to meet Olivia? We're meeting for breakfast. Well, brunch." He smiled, a flicker of anxiety clouding his face.

"Sure." I gulped.

"I know it's short notice. You're busy."

"No. I'd like to."

"We're meeting at Ivan's, at 11:00 a.m."

"The exterminator is due at ten. It'll be tight."

"Whenever you get there is fine, Katelyn."

OMG. I grinned as Don drove away, my heart pounding in my chest.

I took a deep breath, gathered Boots and uncrated him inside. He made a beeline to the sofa, relieved his ordeal with Dr. Katz was over. I scrambled back to the car to make my appointment with pest control.

Chapter 14

My heart still thumped from the flurry of the morning's activity when I arrived at the rehab. The truck from Exterminators R Us was parked on the street, the driver waiting. The side of his truck had a cartoonish illustration of a cockroach on its back.

Nice. Dismayed, I shrugged. *The neighbors will love this.*

The driver bounded from his seat and we met up behind the roll-off dumpster.

"Katelyn Baxter?" the tall thin man held out his hand. "I'm Tim from Exterminators R Us." His grip was firm.

"Yes. I'm Katelyn. I called about a rat."

"Rat, huh. Where?"

"In a box on my kitchen counter."

"Say what?" He lifted his hat and scratched his forehead.

"I called for an inspection to check for possible infestation. It may have been a joke."

"Not very funny." The wiry man frowned.

"I agree." I inhaled, exasperated.

"We've got a special going for inspections. It's more for removal."

"Let me know." DIY rat inspection and removal weren't part of my wheelhouse. I'd leave it to the professionals. I could hardly wait for Wayne to get back. I was sure my handyman could make short shrift of rats, but for now, I was stuck.

"I'll start by checking around the outside of the house."

"Sounds good." Armed with a flashlight, Tim started

inspecting the perimeter while I unlocked the entry.

Inside, I dialed Myra.

"Okay. I've got a few minutes, now. Boots has a clean bill of health from the vet. The exterminator is here. Don wants me to meet his daughter in about an hour."

"Busy girl. He's such a nice man." She chuckled, approving.

"Yes. Myra."

"You don't sound happy."

"Yeah. Not so much," I muttered. My stomach lurched. "What if she hates me?"

"It'll be fine. She'll love you. Why was Eddy at your place this morning?"

"He stopped by with money for the vet and the rent check. He'll help install the mirror in the bathroom at the rehab later today."

"Don and Eddy were there at the same time?" she asked.

I hesitated. "Eddy slept in the guest room. And, yeah. Male bonding and all."

Myra chuckled. "Let me guess, he asked Don about his Corvette?"

"Yep. That's all it took. How's the Hiptown house coming?"

"There's some progress. The contractor appears to have settled any feuds between the subcontractors about working conditions. No reports of missing lumber or tools."

I saw Tim walking around the front picture window, checking the garden level for areas that vermin might gain entry while Myra and I chatted.

"That's great, Myra. You wouldn't want to have a sage burning here, would you?"

"Because of the rat?"

"Because of the DEAD rat," I retorted, and Myra

started laughing.

"Hey, at least you had cute raccoons. This thing was UGLY," I protested. Tim stood at the entry, and I gestured for him to come in. "I have to go."

"Sure. Let's do a cleansing. A dead body is a dead body. Well, not quite. You know what I mean." She chuckled.

Tim waited patiently in the foyer while I finished with Myra. "What did the rat look like?" he asked.

"It was a big, brown rat, about yay big." I showed him the length with my hands. "A Norway rat, I'm told."

"Uh huh. I'll check around inside the downstairs, and inspect the crawl space."

"Knock yourself out." I shrugged.

I futzed upstairs, making a note of how many gallons of paint I'd need for the main floor.

"It doesn't look bad," he announced, returning to the vestibule.

"Good. What does that mean?"

"I don't see any droppings or burrows around the foundation. Nothing in the garden level storage space. Rats like to nest in crawl spaces."

I shuddered, relieved. "So, no influx."

"None, that I see."

"You're sure?"

"Yep."

"Okay." I retrieved my credit card from my bag and paid Tim for his inspection. "Where is a Norway rat typically found?"

"They like sewers. Places where they can get to water. Garbage dumps, cities."

"I imagine a plumber could get one."

"Yep. Pretty easy." Tim looked baffled. He handed me my card. "Thanks for using Exterminators R Us. Call if there's anything else I can do."

"I will." I closed the door behind him, and reflected on Tim's statement about rats. My mind had leaped to Randy when he said rats liked sewers. But why on earth would he leave vermin? We'd had an awkward conversation about Sarah being married to Fernando. Before that, she'd been married to Randy's dad in Arizona. He thought Sarah was found in the bedroom, not the kitchen, as Fernando claimed. None of that meant he'd leave a rat as a warning. Did it?

I put that thought on hold while I took a last-minute pass at my hair and slapped on lip gloss. Locking up, I headed over to Ivan's to meet Don and the daughter who'd found him.

Ivan and Maggie greeted me from behind the front counter.

Katarina waved me to the booth where Don waited. "He is there!" she snapped. I went to the designated booth.

"Thanks," I grumbled under my breath. *No one else could be that bad-mannered and stay employed.*

"Still waiting on Olivia?" I asked, checking the time. It was approaching 11:30.

"Yes. She's young. Likes to sleep in." He looked uncertain, giving him an air of vulnerability. "Go ahead, order. I know you're on a project."

"I'll have coffee while we wait."

"Go ahead, order. I did." He coughed, nervously. "Olivia hasn't been a model of punctuality." He gave a wry smile.

The start of April was cool and overcast with light drizzle. A perfect day for soup or Ivan's chili.

"Okay. Chili sounds good." Ivan's zesty dish was to die for and I was hungry after my adventure with the exterminator. After observing plates of food delivered to other diners, I ordered. Katarina snatched up the menu and bustled off. I looked after her, frowning. Don caught my expression and smirked. We forgot for the moment we were waiting on his daughter.

"What kind of work does Olivia do?"

"She's between jobs," Don said.

"Oh."

"Her mother left her money when she passed, so she's exploring her options, finding herself."

"Nice." *Yeah, right.*

Our food arrived, and we dug in. I savored the blend of spices. *Oh, the food, that's why we come here.* I closed my eyes, relishing the dish and searching for the proper thing to say.

"Olivia's young. Losing a parent is a lot to come to terms with. How old is she?"

"She just turned twenty-one."

I paused, while I did the math, and frowned, "That makes her fourteen years my junior." I stirred the cheese into the chili and kept my expression blank. "She's a baby." *She looked older.* I felt a twinge of protectiveness, motherly. Being without a parent is rough. I tried to kid, saying, "She's just a few years younger, if I stick to my story, that I'm twenty-eight." I cringed at being thirty-five years old. Twenty-nine was a cliché. So, twenty-eight, it was.

"I suppose so. I'm forty-five, I'd have been twenty-four when she was born. I should have known better." He looked regretful and held his coffee cup with both hands, adding, "She appears more mature than her years."

"She had to grow up fast," I nodded. "I suppose she had the birth certificate; her mother gave her a copy?"

"Yes."

"Anything else?" I sipped coffee.

"Like a DNA match?" The words hung in the air while I squirmed under his pointed question.

"I bring you more coffee!" Katarina leaned toward my cup with the coffee carafe and poured. She filled it to the rim, and I winced.

"I don't mean to be nosy, but they can alter documents. These days, you can't be too careful," I protested.

"Yes. If anyone should know that, it's a sheriff." His tone was subdued. "I'll do a DNA test. I haven't wanted to face the possibility she could be a fraud. Someone who wants to take advantage of an unfortunate situation. The death of her mom. Or an old bachelor, like myself."

"It's better for everyone to know the truth. She might have been fed a pack of lies and found you in good faith. And forty-five is not old."

He smiled. "Thank you, Katelyn. That's good to hear." A smile stretched across his face reaching the corners of his eyes. "Even if it comes from someone who fibs about her age."

"No problem," I said, and snickered.

It was twelve-thirty when the server dropped the check on the table with a sniff.

"It looks like Olivia is a no-show," Don said, with a touch of wistfulness.

"Did you tell her I was joining you?"

"Yes. She sounded excited about meeting someone in my life."

I winced, remembering the day I dumped the glass of water into his lap, thinking the worst. The perky red-head was next to him, looking cozy, when I spotted the two. "We could meet up another time?" I suggested brightly. "I don't suppose you have any information on Sarah Anderson's death, you'd want to share?"

"No. I can't discuss an ongoing investigation."

"Yeah. Kind of thought that's what you'd say. I got a bit of good news from the exterminator."

"What's that?"

"My rat was an interloper. There are no signs of an infestation."

"That's great!" He held his up cup in celebration.

"I asked Tim, the pest control expert, where a rat might have come from. He said sewers, garbage, cities."

"Sounds logical." He lowered the cup.

"A plumber would have access to all kinds of rats," I submitted.

"Okay. Where is this going?" He was abrupt.

"My plumber, Randy. Maybe you should question him about the rodent?"

He shook his head. "You think your plumber left you a rat? Why?"

"I'm not sure." I sipped my coffee. "He said his father and Sarah got married when they lived in Arizona. That her body was discovered in the bedroom. Fernando says it was the kitchen."

"How would Randy know?" he asked.

"Maybe someone leaked information from the investigation? Could be a distraction from what really happened?"

"Point investigators in another direction to avoid the truth?" he asked. "Anything is possible."

We made small talk until nearly one o'clock. Don sat back, chaste, "I'll give Olivia a little more time."

"Of course! But I should go. I must paint the bathroom before Eddy comes later to help hang the mirror." I was pushing the recommended time for letting paint dry by installing the mirror so quickly. But I could touch up any dings, and I was eager to get it done.

"Eddy's helping you?"

"It's his payment for letting him sleep over." He raised his eyebrows.

"In the spare room. He drank a couple of beers and didn't want to drive." Yep. I was covering for Eddy, again. He tilted his head and frowned as I yammered.

"Never mind," I said, frustrated, and stood up.

Don's eyes twinkled, and he said, "Thank you for coming. I'll wrangle a meeting with Olivia for another time."

I left Don at the grill. He'd have to satisfy his questions about Olivia with a DNA search. My stomach churned considering I might be the reason for Olivia's no-show. Maybe she remembered the glass of water I tossed in his lap. What was that saying about karma?

Chapter 15

I motored back to Warbler Street.

Myra called while I was taping off the bathroom. "How did it go with Don's daughter?" she asked.

"It didn't. She was a no show."

"Really?" She sounded puzzled.

"Yep."

"That's not good."

"It's not the best," I agreed. "He says he'll do a DNA match."

"Oh, dear. Well, I won't keep you long. When did you want to do the cleansing?" Burning sage was a Native American ritual I'd discovered when I found a dead body at my first flip. I've burned the herb in every project since. There was always a reason for the space to be refreshed, and we were becoming old hands at purging spaces. It gave us a reason for wine too. It had been gratifying to see that Bernie used sage in his rituals, as well.

"Does this evening work? I'm expecting Eddy over to hang the new bathroom mirror? We could celebrate finishing the bathroom and cleanse the kitchen from my deceased rat."

"What did the exterminator say?"

"No infestation here. Someone left the rat."

"Oh my. As a warning?" She gasped.

"Don't know," I said, grimly. "How does five o'clock work? It'll be a welcome diversion."

"Perfect."

I wrapped up painting the bath and placed a fan to speed the drying time. I had a few minutes to spare and cleaned the kitchen and living room before Eddy rang the doorbell at five o'clock. Myra stood beside him, clutching a tote bag filled with sage and candles. He carried Myra's picnic basket loaded with cheese, crackers, wine, and fruit and brought it up to the living room where we dug in.

Myra retrieved crystal stemware from the wicker carrier and poured a glass of wine for each of us.

"Thanks." I nodded. "I appreciate this."

"Yeah. This is boss." Eddy held up his glass, grinning.

"No problem." She brought out a plate for the sage and lit a small bundle. The smoke curled around the offending area in the kitchen and we crossed ourselves.

"Let this be a place of serenity for Katelyn and any bad karma expelled," Myra stated the intention. When the ritual was completed, we raised our glasses in a toast and clicked the crystal, appreciating the clear, simple tone.

"Gee, you're becoming a pro at this." I chuckled.

"I learned from the best," she said in a carefully modulated tone, and smiled.

"Awesome!" Eddy chortled and finished his wine with gusto.

"Let's get the mirror hung," I reminded him, as he helped himself to more food. "After your snack."

"What can I do?" Myra asked.

"You've done so much already. Thank you."

The day had become dark.

"It looks like there's a storm brewing." Myra stood at the picture window, observing the sky. A clap of distant thunder sounded, and a light splatter of raindrops hit the glass.

Eddy picked up one end of the new mirror and we carried it to the bathroom to hang, while Myra packed up the basket. "It's pitch-black. The storm is headed this way," she said. "I should go. Katelyn, are you okay working with Eddy? You're sure you don't need me?"

"Go ahead." I rested my end of the glass on the vanity and hugged her before she took off. Myra was not a hugger, but accepted my gesture stiffly. There was a crack of thunder.

"Are you sure you don't want to wait it out?" I asked.

"I'll be fine," she assured me. "The rain is light. But while there's a lull, I'd better go." Eddy and I watched from the entry as she hurried to her SUV, her jacket hood protecting her hair from droplets.

We positioned the mirror on the wall and stood back, admiring the freshly hung, framed glass. I was pleased we'd hung it without a scratch to the fresh paint. Standing side by side with Eddy reminded me of the time we were young newlyweds and making a home together, and I felt a wisp of nostalgia.

"Thanks, Eddy. It looks wonderful." I gave him a satisfied grin. "But it's best for you to go before the storm gets too bad."

"Yep. Face the music." He grabbed his jean jacket, buttoning up with a fleeting air of resignation.

"Lola?"

"Yep. She wants to talk. I told her I'd call later."

"Uh huh. Good luck with that." "Later" with Eddy could mean anything. He threw his arms around me in a bear hug and grabbed another snack for the road. "This has been great. The mirror looks awesome!" His eyes sparkled, and his long lashes fluttered. He waved the cracker and ambled out.

I made one last tour of our work in the bathroom and gazed at the kitchen counter where the rodent had been. I was satisfied we'd cleared any bad karma. The rain started up again, and I hustled, gathering my bag and locking up. I ran to my car, getting drenched.

I breezed inside my townhome, dropped my messenger bag, and slipped off my jacket to hang in the shower to dry. Boots jumped off the sofa and circled my legs, looking for comforting strokes and chow. I fed him and changed into dry sweats. The storm had gained strength and there was a steady torrent of water pounding the house.

I hurried to the kitchen sliding door and drew the blinds that opened to the patio.

"Quite a storm, huh, Boots?"

I stood at the window and watched the torrential rain slamming the stone pavers. With Wayne and Gillie still in Vegas, and the fourth unit vacant, I was keenly aware of being alone on the dark night. The sky was the inkiest I'd ever seen, with a deep purple hue and heavy rain. I flipped on the patio light. Rain had turned to hail, and the ground was fast covered with white pellets. I closed the blinds to muffle the sound of hail pelting the window.

Kaboom! Another crack of thunder rumbled and lightning flashed behind the closed blinds.

Rap, rap, rap!

"Hey, it's me!" a voice yelled from the hall. I dashed to the door, and opened up to a drenched Eddy.

"What are you doing here?" I exclaimed.

He wore a hangdog expression; his dark hair was wet. Rain trickled from his jacket. His pants and shoes were soaked.

"My truck broke down. The street flooded, and I gunned the engine. The truck stalled. I couldn't get the dang thing started again. Your place was closer than mine. Besides, Lola isn't there. Remember, we're taking a break?"

"OMG." I inhaled. "You can wear my robe while your clothes dry." I dashed to my bedroom closet and took out an oversized, white terry-cloth robe and a towel, and marshaled him to the bathroom.

"I'll check on Myra." I ran to the phone and dialed. When she answered, I breathed a sigh of relief. "You're home!"

"Yes. I just made it. It's a nightmare out there!"

"I'm glad you're safe! Eddy walked here in the downpour. His truck stalled in the flooded streets and he couldn't get started again."

"I'm sorry to hear that. Yes. I'm home. Thanks for calling."

"You stay safe." I hung up. Opening the patio blinds, I resumed my vigil at the window. "OMG!" I watched the hail accumulate. There were three to four inches of pellets outside the window.

With the collar of the fluffy robe up, and wet hair glistening, Eddy joined in watching the angry storm.

"Gosh." He gave a low whistle. "I ain't never seen it this bad. There's going to be a lot of damage from this storm."

"Yeah." My stomach churned, thinking of the rehab on Warbler Street. The siding was vinyl, which was low maintenance, but not immune to hail damage. The Bluebird house had wood siding, more durable, but would likely need paint after this. Roof shingles would be pommeled, too.

The storm raged for another half hour.

We waited it out, hypnotized by flashes of light, fierce winds, and the mound of white pellets on the patio floor. Finally, the wind died down, and the rain and hail quit, leaving an eerie quiet.

"I should check out the houses," I said.

"Wait 'til morning. Not much you can do now."

I considered his advice. Part of me wanted to fix things, ASAP. He was right, though; the insurance people would wait until tomorrow. Maybe I'd get lucky and the damage wouldn't be as bad as I imagined.

"So, the spare room again, Eddy?"

"Thanks, babe."

Babe? Maybe I could get used to the term of endearment?

Chapter 16

The next day the sun melted the mounds of hail. Street flooding receded, manholes were cleared, and travel was safe. I drove Eddy to his truck. He cranked the engine a few times, and the vehicle started. He gave a thumbs up and drove away.

Weather gurus pegged the April storm as the worst in twenty years. Many homes in the area had pitted vinyl exteriors, which gave them the dismal look of a neighborhood that might have been ravaged by gun fire. The damage was bad, although it could have been worse.

After talking to the insurance adjuster, the Warbler renovation, which I thought would be a cream puff project, needed a new roof. With a stroke from Mother Nature, one side of the vinyl siding now needed replacing. Finding a contractor and matching the material would be the biggest challenge, and would mean a serious delay in listing the house.

The roof on the Bluebird house was damaged, and the siding needed paint. So, two insurance claims. Eddy hadn't made any noises about moving out, and his relationship with Lola hadn't affected our rent-to-own agreement. I avoided the subject. I didn't want to think about putting the rental house on the market, too. I had to focus on finishing the renovation.

The luminol arrived. It was a wonder the delivery trucks maintained their schedules during the worst storm in the last two decades. I opened the box with the kit and mixed the spray.

I took the carpet snippets from Fernando's bedroom

and spread them on a piece of paper in my bathroom. I sprayed them with the solution and flipped off the lights to see if the fibers would glow, meaning the stain was blood. Nothing. No glow, no reaction. I tried it a second time with the same results. I was relieved that it wasn't blood. Sarah hadn't bled in the bedroom. He was telling the truth. She must have bled in the kitchen where he'd found her.

I worked feverishly at the rehab, chastened by my glow-in-the-dark experiment, and mortified that I'd suspected Fernando of anything untoward. Randy was wrong. I doubled down on deep cleaning.

A week later, Fernando rang the doorbell.

I answered with wild hair and smudges on my face, wearing my grungiest clothes. He smiled. "You are working hard, yes?"

"I am." I gazed over his shoulder at his house. "Did you have a lot of damage?"

"It is minor. The roof, some painting." He shrugged. "I was lucky." His brown eyes were soft, but puffiness under his eyes gave him a worn appearance.

"Everyone's roofs were damaged. I have to replace the roof and one side of vinyl. It'll be several weeks. Would you like to see the mirror?" I asked.

"Yes. Very much."

I showed him to the main floor bath. The new mirror updated the space and made the room stylish.

"It is an excellent choice. I am happy for such an unfortunate accident."

"It *is* nice. Thank you for replacing the broken one."

"You are welcome. I came to ask if there is something I might help you with, because of the storm damage?"

"Thank you. That's kind of you, but there isn't anything. How are you?"

"I am well."

"Good."

He walked to the exit, paused in the foyer, and commented, "Your dumpster is gone."

"Yes, it is." I nodded. "I had torn out the carpet from the lower level and filled it. Now it's a matter of finishing the cleanup, painting, and new flooring."

"Yes. Fresh carpet is nice. Fast Floors, a company that my Sarah liked, put a new rug in her bedroom after she passed."

I hesitated; my eyebrows rose in an unasked question.

"She had been ill and slept in the guest room. She wanted me to be rested for work. She was very thoughtful." My gut seized, and I worked to keep my emotions in check.

"Of course." I smiled. "When the house is finished, I'll have a few friends in to toast the result. I'll let you know. Do you like wine?"

"It is my favorite." His grin was huge. "Sangria. I enjoy a glass before bedtime. It is soothing."

I had to hide my suspicions from Fernando until I was positive he wasn't involved in his wife's death. I didn't want any problems selling the house. A friendly invitation for wine would disguise my doubt.

Closing the door behind him, I muttered to myself, "Sarah didn't sleep in the master bedroom. She'd been in another room. That spot on the rug I tested was probably red wine. Curses."

Frustrated, I dialed Myra. "Remember, I told you about my luminol test?"

"Yes. You said you'd test the carpet from Fernando's."

"Well. I did. No glow."

"That's good."

"I thought so too. But he was just here."

"Yes?"

"He said that Sarah slept in another bedroom because she was sick."

"Makes sense," she commented.

Silence. "No, no. Don't go there, Katelyn Baxter," she warned me. "Don't go snooping again."

"It wouldn't matter. Fernando already replaced the rug in the room where she slept."

"So, any evidence of blood is gone. Best to leave it be," she urged.

"I wonder what Dewey would say?" I mused aloud. My new favorite carpet store proprietor may have some information.

"Katelyn!" she admonished.

"Just curious," I responded in a noncommittal tone.

"Uh huh." She didn't sound convinced.

To expedite the repairs, I went with the recommended contractors from the insurance gurus. They replaced both roofs within the month. While I waited for the vinyl siding to be matched and delivered, I focused on completing the inside.

In early May, I met with Dewey. He was calm and confident, answering all my questions about the carpet I chose as he measured each space. I admired his professionalism and said so, as he detailed the numbers. He paused and grinned, "Floors are my life."

Pleased, I said, "I got your name from Randy, the plumber. He recommended you. He mentioned that you replaced flooring at a neighbor's place?"

"Yes, I did. Just across the street, Fernando Garcia's. A bedroom. Carpet was a mess. Wife had spilled a bottle of red wine and couldn't get the stains out. The wine sat far too long. Her husband was eager to fix it."

"Uh huh." Bells rang in my mind.

"It was a shame to hear she'd passed," he added.

"Yes. I'd just started the renovations here when all heck broke loose and the emergency responders removed her body."

"I believe they're still investigating?" he asked.

"Yes."

I gave Dewey a deposit for the new carpet and we shook on the deal. He left, saying he'd call for an installation date when the flooring arrived in about ten to fourteen working days.

Chapter 17

Two weeks later, I returned to the rehab after purchasing supplies from the home store to find new siding had been delivered and stacked by the driveway. Ecstatic, I phoned the office to speak to the contractor. I talked to the job coordinator, and asked about the delivery.

"They'll be out within the week to do the work," the young man said. "The waste container will be delivered later today."

"Do we know what day they'll install the siding?"

"Nope. It's a small job and they'll fit it in between bigger projects."

I pressed the young man, "I want to be here. Let me know."

"We'll give you a heads up."

"Good." Satisfied, I clicked off. Pleased the house would be back to pristine in short order, I continued painting the interior. The month of June was fast approaching, daylight was getting longer, the sun brighter, and the place was becoming a gem with fresh paint. I was psyched about the siding installation and the new flooring on order.

Three days later, I parked in front of the rehab. A pickup truck and other vehicles blocked the driveway. Puzzled, I observed the men tearing off the exterior. As one man removed the vinyl, another worker disposed of the pieces in the refuse container.

I gasped and jumped out of the car.

"What are you doing?" I stared, open-mouthed.

"Katelyn Baxter? You're the owner?" A third man, a

towhead, yelled from the top of the ladder.

"Yes, I am!" I glared.

"I'm Paul," he called out as he descended the ladder. He was tall and lean with firm biceps. "I'm the crew supervisor. We're replacing the siding."

"Paul." I choked. "It doesn't come off the front." I gestured at the wood framing.

"What?" he was skeptical. The workers looked up from hauling material to the roll-off container. They stopped with their loads and stared at me, the crazy woman freaking out, and to Paul for guidance.

"Follow me to the west side." I led him, my face burning and shoulders tensed.

He shuffled behind me, and took a moment to bark out "stop work" to the laborers. Both men shrugged, and dropped the ripped pieces.

I stopped at the side that displayed pits from the hail storm.

He surveyed the damage. With a hint of chagrin, "I'll call the office."

"Do that!" Defeated, I grumbled under my breath, "Who are these people?" and headed to the car to get supplies. I'd just dropped my bags in the entry when the doorbell rang.

Paul stood on the stoop with his back to me. He pivoted, and said with a sheepish expression, "They meant for the material to go to another address."

I blinked. "This isn't my order?"

"No."

"What now?"

"We'll make it right. We have to order more siding. It's on back order, so it'll take time."

"How long?"

"It'll be six to eight weeks. If we can still get it. There's limited supply. Many houses need to be resided. It's always better if you do everything. Change colors."

Again, I was struck speechless and sputtered. "No. I don't think so."

"Well, it may take as long as two months."

"You're not leaving it this way!"

"We'll put the old pieces that aren't damaged back." He grimaced at my obvious angst. "I apologize. The office staff gave us the wrong address."

I shut the door in Paul's face. *Yeah. It's always the office that screws up.*

Eventually, the sounds of hammers dwindled to silence. One by one, vehicles sped off. I ventured out to view the front of the house. It had all the earmarks of a slum dwelling, with bare wood at the top, and chunks of siding missing.

"There is a problem, yes?" I jumped at the voice behind me.

"Yes. Fernando." I sighed. "They were supposed to do the west side," and I pointed, frustrated.

"*Ay caramba*! I am sorry."

"Me, too." My gut seized as I surveyed the mess. How was I ever going to get this rehab to market? If the siding was available, delivery would take months, well beyond my time frame. I couldn't afford to replace all the material. Besides, it had been in great condition.

"I have sangria?" His soft eyes were sympathetic. "I would be happy to share a bottle? It will look better after a glass of vino."

I checked my watch; it was nearly five o'clock. "That's a great idea. I'll lock up." In the back of my mind, I briefly considered how my visit to Fernando's might look to any nosy neighbor. I reasoned; it was a friendly gesture for a trying day. Surely anyone would understand. I didn't know if he had anything to do with his wife's death. And the curious neighbor in me wanted another look at the inside of his house.

Shaking my head at the day's debacle, I headed over after locking up.

"Please, come in." He waved me to the table and gratefully I sank into a chair. Two glasses of liquid comfort awaited. He kept a clean kitchen. On my first visit, I'd been inside briefly to get the check for the busted mirror, and searched the master bedroom. There were no smudges visible on the stainless appliances. All dishes were out of sight in the cupboards or dishwasher. The counters were clear of clutter.

"Here is a toast to better times." He held up his stemware, and I clicked my glass against his. His demeanor was soothing, and I almost believed it. My eyes held his for a brief minute.

"Amen to that."

He grinned. The jangle of the telephone interrupted our toast.

"Please, excuse me." He rose and answered the phone in the living room. I tuned out his muted conversation, pondering the day's events. My mind flitted to the grim thought that Sarah had taken her last breaths in the guest room. I shifted in the wooden chair at the country-style dining set, and scanned the area for any evidence of the tragedy. I itched to find the bedroom Sarah had slept in to search for any clues to her death.

Grimacing, I held my head, resting elbows on the table. In the process, I jostled the glass, and spilled wine over the table. "Dang it." I grabbed a sponge from the sink to mop up the mess, wiped the spill, then threw the sponge back. It hit the floor.

"I am such a klutz," I grumbled. I reached for the item and glanced up. Stunned, I stared at the spots. On the underside of the cupboard were dots of red. Spatter.

"So sorry to leave you alone. It was not important." He shrugged; his brows rose at seeing me stooped by the sink.

I rose and said, "I'm sorry, my wine spilled. I was cleaning up." I rinsed the sponge, keeping my expression still.

"No worries. We have a bottle. Please leave it." He came behind me and took the scrubber. Our hands met. His touch was warm, he leaned in, and gently kissed me on the cheek. I froze.

Eek!

"I'll leave now," I whispered, shaking.

"I do not mean to scare you," he murmured into my hair.

Too late.

"I need to go," I mumbled, panicky.

"No, please. Do not go. Do not be afraid," he protested. I broke loose from his spell, grabbed my handbag and ran from the kitchen to the safety of my car. What just happened? Was he out of his mind, kissing me? Was it a small sign of affection I was blowing out of proportion? Was it blood spatter I'd seen beneath the cabinet? I gunned the car and sped home.

Chapter 18

I lost no time dialing Myra after blowing in from my encounter with Fernando.

While she and I dissected what had transpired with the renovation and my encounter with the neighbor, I fed Boots. He yowled in the background while we talked.

"It might be a marinara sauce from cooking or spray from a can of cola?"

I responded evenly, "Or, he could have conked Sarah on the head. The blood hit the cabinet, and he missed it when he cleaned. The medical examiner's report said blunt force injury."

"When you put it that way . . ." she reflected. "But Fernando wasn't home. He found her when he came home for lunch. Someone else could have dealt the blow and missed cleaning the spots. How can you know?" She read my mind. "No. No more luminol."

"Humm."

"How on earth would you get in? If it is blood, that still doesn't prove he did it."

"Maybe." I was stumped, and went on to the other drama, my contractor.

"What? Who is this contractor?" She gasped and laughed.

"Yeah. I know," I said, sighing. "It's a huge snag in the renovation's progress."

Rap, rap.

I frowned and looked through the peephole. "Myra, I have to go. Eddy's here."

"Eddy?"

"Yep." I disconnected, and opened the door.

He grinned, and his eyes sparkled. "I drove past the Warbler Street house. Love what you've done with the place," and he let out a belly laugh.

"It isn't funny!" I saw the glint of laughter in his expression, recalled the wrecked facade, and snickered, chortling, "It'd be funnier if it wasn't my project." I sobered up. "How's Lola?"

"Still on a break. How 'bout dinner at Ivan's? My treat."

"Great. I'll get ready." Spending time with Eddy would be a welcome diversion. He knew me. Lord knows what or where Don was. Was he still sorting out Felicity and Olivia? Did he see Eddy as a rival? All I knew was that I was keen to get out.

While I showered and changed, the phone rang.

I leaped to answer and got to it before Eddy picked up the extension in the kitchen. "Wayne! When will you be back?" I bit my lip, hearing how eager my voice sounded.

"Hey, Kiddo." His deep voice soothed me. "We're thinking the end of the month. What's up? Somethin' wrong?"

"You won't believe it; the contractor removed the wrong siding."

"Whaaaaat? Who the heck are these guys?" He whistled, then guffawed. His laughter slowed to a chuckle, and I said, "Go ahead, laugh. I miss you."

"We'll be home 'for ya know it. Me and Gillie are having a great time."

"I hope you have the time of your lives. Don't worry about the rehab." I tried to sound positive, given the day's events. I took a deep breath, and asked, "Will you move in with Gillie, or is she moving in with you?"

"I was gonna tell ya! We're gettin' our own place."

"Oh?" I asked, stemming my disappointment they'd be moving.

"We're gonna keep our places, too."

"All right?"

"We put in an offer on Ariel's old place." Ariel was the haughty neighbor who'd met her end in the fourth townhouse. Wayne and I had done the renovation with a generous contract from her wealthy family. Her relatives hadn't sold or rented out the unit yet.

"That sounds like a plan." I was relieved.

"Yep. That way, we keep our own space, and a place that's ours. Convenient."

"Sure. That makes sense." Sort of. The seniors had lived on their own for several years. Merging households could be a challenge.

"Give it a trial run, anyway. We can always sell later."

"Sure."

They weren't kids. I didn't know if that would be my solution to combining households. But it would be wonderful having him back to work on my projects. With his steady hand, I doubted the fiasco that had transpired today would have happened if he'd been there.

I hung up, did a jig, then finished getting ready to go out with Eddy.

Seated at Ivan's, I sipped a glass of chardonnay and filled Eddy in on the happenings. Snickering, his eyes flashed with mirth, and he tried to stifle his laughter. After drinking vino, I could appreciate the preposterous turn of events and dissolved into laughter along with him. I regained my composure, and asked, "So, how is it with you and Lola?"

"Like I said, she's taking a breather." He shrugged.

"So, no change in the status of our rental agreement." I studied his expression.

"Nope." He avoided my gaze. "What's happening

with Don?"

"It's complicated." I gulped. He'd never asked about the sheriff. It was uncharted territory, best left unexplored, and changed the subject. "After the siding fiasco, Fernando invited me over for a drink."

He frowned.

"It wasn't anything. He saw the siding upset me." I decided not to tell him about Fernando's kiss. It was probably nothing.

"Uh huh." He grimaced.

"When I was in the kitchen, I saw marks, maybe blood spatter, under a cabinet."

"Under the cabinet? How? What were you doing?" He frowned and shifted, crossing his arms.

"I spilled my wine and missed the sink when I tossed the sponge. As I retrieved it, I looked up. That's when I saw the spots."

He let loose a low whistle, and asked, "Where was he?"

"He was on a call in the living room."

"Have they figured out what happened to his wife?"

"Not that I know of."

"Kate, stay away from his place and tell the police what you saw."

"You might be right. But what if it's just spaghetti sauce?"

He shrugged and reached for my hand. I clasped his, wishing life was simple again, like when we were teenagers.

"Let's go." He stood and threw down some bills.

Silent and pensive, he drove home. He left me at my front door, saying, "Gotta figure out what's going on with Lola." He leaned towards me, and his lips brushed my forehead.

Eddy was growing up.

Chapter 19

The next day, convinced that Eddy was right, I decided to tell Don about what I'd seen in Fernando's kitchen. I worked up the courage to head over to the police station. I considered how to broach the subject as I drove past the drugstore, antique shops, Crocus Heights Bank, and parked in the lot across from the station. I entered the cop shop with a plan—I'd be direct.

The sheriff's office door was open, and he sat at his desk, staring at a computer monitor. Pausing outside the entrance, I coughed to get his attention.

"Katelyn? What brings you here?" He glanced up with a welcoming smile, and I went straight to the subject.

"I saw something at Fernando Garcia's house that the police might want to investigate."

His eyebrows rose. "Shut the door." He waved me to the chair opposite his desk. I eased into the seat and squirmed, aware his body dwarfed me.

"You were inside Garcia's place?" He crossed his arms and sat back, staring.

"Yes. It was an innocent glass of wine," I protested.

His brows knitted; he continued his gaze.

"I'd had a run-in with the siding contractor." He stayed silent, studying me. I gulped.

He cleared his throat, sat up, and asked tersely, "What did you see?"

I flushed, and responded, "Brownish red spots that resembled blood under the kitchen cabinet, next to the sink."

"Our investigators combed the kitchen. I think they would have found blood spatter." He appeared wary and shifted in his chair.

I bristled at his tone. “They could have missed it. I’m just telling you what I saw.”

“Uh huh.” He leaned back, and laced his hands behind his head. “I think it’s best you stay away from your neighbor. His wife’s death is still under investigation. I don’t want you in the middle of a case.”

“I understand.” My voice was flat, and I bit my lower lip.

He frowned; his blue eyes sharpened. “You have all the doors locked while you work. Correct?”

A twinge of doubt niggled. *Had I?*

“Yes. Any leads on my rat?” I sparred.

“None yet. Reports are still coming in about a prowler in the neighborhood.” He rubbed his temple. My dig had hit a spot. “In the meantime, let the police do the investigating.” His eyes strayed to his screen; I did an eye-roll and stood up. I wanted to ask about Olivia, but hesitated.

He must have read my mind, because his tone was softer. “I’ve sent in my DNA along with Olivia’s. I should know the results in about a week.”

“Oh. How does Olivia feel about you doing the test?” I shuffled my feet, embarrassed.

“Not good. She won’t answer my calls or texts.”

“I’m sorry. She’s probably upset that you doubt her. It’s good you told her. You could have ordered the test without her knowledge.”

“Yes. I suppose that’s so.” His eyes misted, and he coughed. “Should have done it right away. Before we got comfortable.”

“It’s better for her to know the truth, too. It’s the right thing to do,” I ventured.

“Yes. The correct thing isn’t always the easiest.” He smiled wryly.

When I left, he was staring at the computer screen

again. I felt like a heel for suggesting he should verify Olivia's claim that she was his father. Would I ever learn to mind my own business?

On my way to the Warbler rehab, I passed Randy's Plumbing truck in the driveway at a nearby residence. I pulled into my drive, noting that Fernando's truck was parked across the street.

"He must be home for lunch," I muttered. The dismal view of the front of the renovation taunted me, and I grumbled "idiots" as I entered. I dropped my messenger bag on the kitchen counter and headed to the attached garage.

It was time I did some landscaping work. I grabbed a rake and cleared out the beds in front and in back. There were bits of siding scattered about, and the plants had taken a beating from the contractors tearing off material. I placed the remnants in the dumpster. While I raked, the sheriff's car pulled into Fernando's driveway.

Covertly, I watched the sheriff knock. He nodded towards me while waiting on the stoop for Fernando. He cocked his head to one side, his brows rose, surveying the exterior of the renovation. I shrugged, catching his gawk. Fernando opened the door, and the sheriff went in.

About fifteen minutes later, Don emerged from Fernando's, and trotted to where I raked grass bordering the driveway.

"Katelyn." He tugged his hat.

"Sheriff." I addressed him formally, given he was in uniform, and it appeared he'd followed up on my observation at Fernando's.

"Stay out of this investigation," he said, his jaw firm.

I faced him and straightened to my nearly five and a half feet. "Did you see the droplets?"

"Yes." He was terse.

"And?"

"Do as I say, keep away from Garcia's residence, and out of police work."

"You're not going to tell me?"

"All I have to say," he paused, "is that marinara sauce makes a mess."

"That's all it was?" I rested the rake's handle against my shoulder, frowning.

"I repeat, do not get involved with this case." He pushed his sunglasses up and gave me a steely gaze.

"So, it wasn't blood?" I asked stubbornly.

"Have a pleasant afternoon." He turned and hiked to the squad, tossing one last glare as he sped off.

I raked furiously, grumbling as I whacked at the lawn. Out of the corner of my eye, I viewed Fernando exit his house, get into his pickup, and drive away.

Had Fernando seen Don talking to me?

I collected the piles of dry turf, deposited them into a garbage bag, and left the waste at the curb. I retreated to the garage, propped the rake, and hit the remote. Inside, I marched upstairs to the bathroom to clean up.

"Oh, dang it all to heck!" After a few more curses, I stared at the mess. The shiny, new mirror Eddy and I had hung, lay on the floor, shattered into a million pieces. The frame was busted at the corners. Sighing, I called Don on my cell and waited outside for his return.

"It's vandalism," he said. "Someone ripped it off the wall. If the mirror wasn't secure and fell, it would crack, but not shatter."

"That's what I thought." I surveyed the mess. He scribbled on a notepad. "Anything else?"

"I don't know. I left when I saw the broken glass."

"Good. Let's see if there's any more damage."

"Okay." We started with the upper level and circled

through the empty bedrooms and back. I shook my head. "Doesn't look like any other breakage."

"Let's check out the lower level." The floors were bare, awaiting carpet from Fast Floors. Wide windows let in light. I noted the dust, another cleaning project I'd tackle after they installed the new carpet. At the far side of the family room, there was an access panel to the crawl space. Don spotted the entry, removed the door, leaned in, and said. "Looks clear."

I walked the hallway, opened a small coat closet, viewed the two small bedrooms, and the small bath. I stopped at the bathroom entry and stared at the toilet. The lid was up. My habit was to keep the lid down. I stepped two feet into the room. My heart sped up, and I hyperventilated, staring at the toilet. The long tail of a rodent hung over the edge of the bowl. I screamed and let out a quick gasp. Don came running and stopped behind me.

"Should get the exterminator and call a plumber," he said. Backing up, I fumbled my way around his body and stared from the entry.

I peeked around his bulk, "Oh, double dang!" I shuddered.

"The animal's dead, Katelyn." He chuckled. "Can't hurt anything now. Rats can enter through the toilet. Call the plumber."

"But I always shut the lid!" It was routine; a quirk of mine.

"Then someone wanted you to find it, sooner than later." He shot me a quick glance and stepped back.

"That does it!" I shouted, and headed upstairs.

"If you get a bag, I'll take it out," he called. "Bring gloves, if you have them?"

I rummaged through drawers and found two empty bags saved from my home store shopping. I snatched up a pair of yellow rubber gloves, detoured to the garage, grabbed a garden hoe, and headed to the bath.

"Here." I offered the items.

He slipped on the gloves, took the tool and lifted the rodent into the bag. He stood up, and double bagged the vermin. "I hope you know; this goes above and beyond the call of duty." He tied the package.

"Thank you," I said, "but the exterminator said there wasn't any sign of infestation."

"I'll add it to my report. Wouldn't hurt to have him do another check. A plumber can fix the toilet so it doesn't happen again."

"Yeah. I guess." My stomach sunk; more bills. "You think the rat swam through the sewer pipes? If the exterminator thinks not, then whoever left the rodent meant it as another warning."

Don didn't answer. That was the only confirmation I needed.

He dusted for prints around the toilet and on the mirror. We each took pictures of the damage. The glass wasn't a big enough item to submit to insurance. Its destruction felt like another threat, like the rodents.

After he left, I locked up, wondering who was trying to scare me, and why. What had I gotten myself into? I reviewed when I'd left the doors open, and couldn't recall any time, except for when I did the outdoor work. Today? It was unlikely. I'd been outside, and it was broad daylight. If not then, someone must have a key, or knew how to get past locked doors. Then I remembered how fast Wayne had jimmied the lock to Ariel's old townhouse the night she was found dead.

If he could get past a secured door, someone else could do the same.

Chapter 20

I called Randy of Randy's Plumbing. Once again, he picked up, and I marveled that a plumber would answer his calls and not let them go to voice mail. I explained about the rodent and he responded in a calm tone with a charge, and added, "I can be there in an hour."

"Great." It bothered me he didn't seem put off by the job, and asked, "Does this kind of thing happen a lot?"

"No. It's not that common."

"Okay."

I locked the door behind me while I raked the front lawn and waited for Randy. I wasn't ready to tackle cleaning up another mirror and wanted some space between me and the damage. While I groomed the lawn, I surreptitiously watched Fernando's place. I hoped he hadn't put it together—that my visit had prompted a call from the sheriff. His truck was gone, and I presumed the coast was clear. I felt sheepish that Don had found nothing more sinister than marinara sauce, and kept my focus on the fact that I'd need another mirror and the charges I'd rack up from a plumber, and an exterminator.

Randy pulled into the drive exactly an hour later. He stepped out of his truck and I stopped my lawn work.

"Hey, Randy." I laid the rake down and brushed my jeans.

"Which toilet had the varmint?" His mouth puckered, fighting a smirk.

"The basement. What can you do to prevent a rat in the toilet?" I asked, resigned.

"I'll install a special flap that closes before a rat can get through the sewer pipe."

"Sounds good." I unlocked the door, and he followed.

"You always lock up when you're outside?" he asked.

"When I'm inside too." I glanced back at him, sensing his presence behind me.

"Smart." His gaze was cool. *Why did he ask and why did he notice?* Suddenly, I was uneasy in his presence. He noticed my nervousness, and said, "Stuff can happen any time, in any neighborhood. Best to keep everything secure."

I hesitated. "Yes. I've had some vandalism."

"That's tough." He nodded, sympathetic.

"It's not good." I showed him to the lower bath.

"I'll get started. Should do both toilets," he said.

"Yes." I'd already factored in two toilets. "So, double the rate you quoted?"

"Two toilets, two flaps."

"Yep." I sighed. Randy didn't work cheap. "I'll leave you to your job."

I headed upstairs to clean up the broken mirror, cursing as I collected the pieces, keeping an ear out for Randy's progress. After double bagging the shards of glass, sweeping, then damp mopping to get any stray pieces, Randy appeared at the entry.

"Ready to do this toilet?" I asked.

"Yep." He had his tool kit in hand and waited for me to leave. He'd worked up a sweat and removed his hat. His bald spot shined with perspiration, and his shirt was soaked.

While he worked, I called Tim from the Exterminator R Us company. He promised to be out the next day.

I struggled to make small talk with Randy. I was curious about his relationship with Fernando and Sarah, his father's ex-wife.

"Did you live in Mesa?"

"Yep."

"You worked there too?"

"I worked with my dad until the market went bust. It forced dad to sell to Vinnie."

"Who's Vinnie?"

"Vincent Deala," he grimaced. "He was my dad's partner. A crook."

"Oh?" I waited for an explanation. He pursed his lips.

"Must have been tough on your dad?"

"Yep." He frowned.

"So, Vinnie still owns the business?"

"Guess so." He shrugged and let the toilet lid slam.

"Tough times." Randy must be bummed, if he'd thought he'd take over the business from his father. Did Randy Sr. really want to sell? "Do you like Minnesota?"

"It's okay. Hard to build a business again." He shot me a cool look.

"I get that. You seem to do okay. I see your truck around the neighborhood a fair amount."

"Uh huh." He collected his tools, stood up, and adjusted his hat. "I'll get your invoice."

"Sure." I waited in the entry, credit card in hand, while he went to his truck to figure my bill. He stood at the van's passenger's door, writing. When he finished, he ripped off a form and met me. I handed him my card, "I know. There's a fee for credit cards."

"Yep." He ran my card, and I signed off.

Not very chatty.

Tim came the next morning, and I breathed a sigh of relief after he inspected the lower level and outside grounds and didn't find droppings or nests for Norway rats. That meant Randy's visit likely stopped any swimming rodents. It was worth the money for the peace of mind.

"You could have a prankster in the neighborhood." He charged my card for another visit.

"Maybe." I bit my bottom lip and frowned.

He left, and I searched the perimeter of the residence, filling in around exposed pipes with a white foam, and leaving boxes of rat poison as a precaution.

I gnashed my teeth and bought another mirror for the bathroom. Eddy helped install the unframed simple plate glass.

"Looks great, Kate."

"I guess. I'd liked the ritzy frame on the broken mirror." I grimaced and threw up my hands.

"This way, the new owner can put their finishing touches on the home." He grinned. "Sometimes, you have to let it go."

"Yeah." I sighed, viewing the bathroom. I couldn't afford an expensive mirror with the additional bills and delays in the project. Time was money, and the months had flown. The longer the dwelling stayed unoccupied, the costlier the renovation.

I worked several nights into the wee hours of the morning to finish cleaning and painting. It was during these marathon work efforts that I heard noises and dismissed them as part of an overtired and overactive imagination. I wasn't going down the path of anything or anyone haunting this rehab. I had to keep my eyes on the prize. A finished home listed and sold.

In the early morning hours of one of my last long sessions, I heard sounds of shouting. I went to the picture window and peered out. Randy's van was parked in Fernando's driveway and the two men were arguing. I crept downstairs and opened the front door a crack to hear the commotion. The surrounding homes were dark and quiet while the men shouted.

"You threw everything out?" Randy yelled; his voice ringing. "You bastard!"

"She wanted to be free of the life she had with your father!"

"You lie! She was ready to leave you! My father wants her stuff!"

"The boxes are gone. Sarah would never leave me. You are a sick man!"

I held my breath and listened. A gust of wind caught the screen door, and it flew open with a creak and slammed shut. The noise caught the two men's attention, and they looked over. I pretended not to notice their argument and latched the screen. Randy marched to his vehicle and drove away, agitated, mouthing what appeared to be profanities. Fernando saw my retreat and went inside.

I thought about their argument and remembered the containers Fernando had disposed of in the first dumpster. They'd looked like mementos from earlier years in Sarah's life. What if she'd packed them to take to a new life? Maybe she didn't mean to dispose of them, as Fernando claimed? Don had taken the cartons for his investigators to sort through for possible clues to her death. I'd heard nothing about the contents, and it was doubtful I would, given he wouldn't disclose anything about the investigation.

I called Randy later that morning. He answered on the second ring.

"Hi, I have another job; could you inspect the hose to the washing machine?" By now, my calls to Randy were probably keeping his business afloat.

"Is the hose cracked?"

"No. Not that I can see. I'm having carpet installed, and the washer is in an area next to the new flooring. I want to be sure the hoses are good before they install the new carpet."

"Every homeowner should have hoses and faucets inspected annually."

"Sure." Another thing to do.

"If you need work, I'll give you an estimate then. I can be there about four o'clock today."

"Perfect."

Later that afternoon, I watched for Randy's truck.

"You again," he commented, and I smiled. He was all business as he examined the hose to the machine and did a routine inspection of other faucets. I trailed him as he checked all the connections. "It's a good thing you called."

"Oh?"

"This faucet is leaking." We were in front of the house and he pointed to a trickle of water after he closed the spigot. While I observed the dribble, he stared past my shoulder at Fernando's. His lip curled, and his focus narrowed.

"Oh?" *Figures.* I'd just turned on the main control to the outdoor faucets for watering the lawn and bushes. I ignored his distracted manner.

"I can change it now." He pursed his lips.

"Sure." He heard me sigh. "It'll cost you a bunch more on the utility bill, if you don't fix it."

"No. Go ahead." *Ka-ching, ka-ching.*

I hung out and trimmed bushes while he fixed the leaky faucet.

"I suppose you get into a lot of muck and pests as a plumber?"

"Yep." He brought out a wrench from a toolbox.

"Like the sewer rat in my toilet?" I clipped a branch from an evergreen shrub.

"Yep." He hesitated and tightened the faucet.

"You do jobs all over the city?"

"Yep." He inhaled, frowning at the connection. Randy was not a talker.

When he finished, he straightened, and said, "I'll get your bill."

I went inside, retrieved my credit card and met him at his van.

"So, does your dad still live in Arizona? Their summers are beastly hot," I said, trying to make polite conversation while he ran my charge.

"No. He hated Arizona. He's a Minnesota native; loves the four seasons."

"Oh? What kind of work does he do?" He had loosened up, and I wanted to keep him talking.

"Retired. Does odds and ends kind of jobs."

That sounded vague, but I went for it. "I could use a handyman."

"I'll tell him." He relaxed.

"Do that. Does he live nearby?"

"No." He was brusque and handed off the receipt. "Thank you for your business." He shook my hand and motored away, making a final stare toward the neighbor's house. Randy wasn't giving me much information. He'd started to talk about his father. Not so much about his work. Later, I would Google.

By the time he left, I was exhausted. It was dinnertime, and I needed to feed Boots, clean up, eat, and research Randy Jackson, Sr. I won't lie; mostly, I wanted to snooze. It'd been a restless night, and I was operating on about three hours of sleep. That morning, I'd fed the cat, ate a quick breakfast, filled up on strong coffee, and hustled back to the house for more chores.

I glanced in my rearview mirror and backed out of the driveway, smacking into the side of Fernando's red pickup. The impact jolted me.

"OMG." I jumped out and stared at the creased fender. "I can't believe it. I looked!" In my haste to leave, I didn't see the truck. Lack of sleep does funny things to your vision.

"It is okay, Katelyn. Insurance will cover it." Fernando had heard the impact inside his home and ran out to the vehicle.

"OMG, I didn't see it! Isn't it usually in the drive?" I protested, flustered.

"Yes. I parked on the street. I will sealcoat the driveway today."

"I'm sorry. I'll get my insurance information." I grabbed my messenger bag and dug out the card.

"I will give you mine." He slipped his wallet from the back pocket of his pants, and flipped through the clear holders. We scribbled our data on scraps of paper from my purse.

"You have pictures?" I glimpsed a photo of a blonde woman. "I love pictures."

"Yes. It is my Sarah." He opened his wallet, displaying the worn photo. "I'm afraid it is old."

"No problem. She's beautiful." My stomach churned. It was the same picture I'd taken from the bins he'd dumped. But the man Sarah had posed with had been clipped out.

"We were planning to take a new picture, but time got away from us. It is sad. Time is fleeting and precious."

"You said you and Sarah had been married a year?" I kept my expression neutral. *Plenty of time to take a new picture.*

"Ahh," he sighed, "we were married for many years, in each other's eyes."

I frowned.

"Our living together was commitment enough for us."

"But it wasn't a legal marriage?" I guessed.

"A license is just a piece of paper." His sad eyes

implored.

I groaned inwardly. As a single woman, I'd heard that line a few times.

"She was lovely." I smiled, meeting his gaze.

I slid in behind the wheel of my Ford with the newly dented corner and drove home. *What is it with men who don't want to make a legal commitment?*

After a hot shower and dinner, I repeated my thoughts to Myra over the telephone. I'd settled in on the sofa with my computer, ready to Google Randy Jackson.

"I agree with you. A man should commit legally to a woman he loves." I felt vindicated and fully supported. She added, "Perhaps she didn't care to commit."

"Okay."

"Like you with Eddy?" She reminded me of his casual marriage proposal before Lola moved into the Bluebird Street residence. My anxiety had risen, remembering our fast and furious year as teenage newlyweds, and all I could think was, *Noooooo.*

"You think Sarah didn't *want* to marry Fernando?"

"It's possible."

"Great." I hung up. I recalled an earlier conversation with Fernando about Sarah. He had lied. He wasn't Sarah's third husband. He may have been the third man she'd lived with. Maybe they'd planned to marry, and she had backed out? What else had he lied about? And there was Randy's confrontation about Sarah's possessions. Fernando claimed she'd wanted to get rid of the boxes, and tossed them in the dumpster. Sarah's death had genuinely wounded him, and his eyes misted when he talked about her. Was he embarrassed that she didn't want to marry once he'd brought her to Minnesota? Maybe I was being paranoid. I've been accused of worse.

I Googled Randy Jackson and followed the bread crumbs to people associated with him. Randy Jackson, Sr. was listed in Arizona and Minnesota. That had the ring of a snowbird. It was June. Randy's father should be back in Minnesota.

Chapter 21

I spent the next morning trimming bushes around the renovation. The day warmed while I worked; I slipped off my hoodie and left it on the front stoop, then went back to my task. I lugged the wood ladder around the back to get at a willow tree. After I finished clipping stray branches, I returned to the steps, about to enter the house.

"What the heck is this?" I grabbed my bundled sweatshirt and unfolded it. "A fish? It's a dead fish!" I dropped the shirt. "Eewee! It smells!" I shuddered. Chilled, I dug out my cellphone and called Don. "You have to see this," I sputtered, panicked.

"See what?" he asked. "Never mind, I'm in the neighborhood." He drove in, and met me at the steps. Leaning over, he flipped a corner of the sweatshirt, and studied the object. Stroking his chin, he said, "It's an Asian carp. They're found at the river."

I winced, "Remember when you said the rat was a brown Norway rat, and I said I didn't give a fig about its ancestry?"

"Yes?"

"Same deal."

"Yes. But someone could be sending you a message."

"What?" It puzzled me. "Why on earth would someone wrap a fish in my shirt and leave it on my steps?"

"Don't know. It's a sign—'swimming with fishes,'—as in someone might want you dead. Like in the *Godfather* movies, where the character receives a dead fish. It could be a threat."

"That's a mob thing. Okay, now you're just plain freaking me out."

"I want you to be aware of what's happening here. I'll make a report and beef up patrols. We're still getting reports of prowlers."

"Good grief. Are there really mobsters? In sleepy Crocus Heights?"

"Organized crime is still around. It may be disguised as an ordinary business to launder money from illegal dealings."

"Like drugs?"

"Yes. But let's not get carried away. It could be a joke." He massaged his temple. "How's Eddy?"

"It's not Eddy." As much as he could be a thorn in my side, he knew better. He'd be the one swimming with the fishes, if he thought leaving a dead carp was funny.

"You're sure?" He looked at me, skeptical.

"Yes. I'll ask him, but it's not Eddy." I shrugged.

"Okay. I'll take the fish." He went to his car and came back with a paper sack.

"Please!" I watched him snap a photo and bag the fish with the shirt. "No need to return the sweatshirt." I winced.

"No problem." he smiled.

"What kind of legitimate business would be a front?" I asked.

"All kinds—bars, restaurants, real estate, the construction trades."

"Like plumbers?"

"Yes, and electricians, painters, framers, carpenters, you name it."

"Well, as long as we narrow it down."

"Glad to see you still have a sense of humor. It must've been a shock."

"Yeah." I sighed. "Thanks."

"I'll take this in. You know the drill." He gave me a stern look.

"No private investigating," I said.

"What else?"

"Keep the doors locked," I recited.

Don left, clutching the smelly bundle, and loaded it in the trunk. He waited, expectantly.

I gave a salute, closed the door, and threw the deadbolt. I headed upstairs to the main level and surveyed the premises. It was coming together, with deep cleaning, fresh paint, and ready for carpet. Why would anyone want me dead? What had I gotten into with this project? It wouldn't matter how good this rehab looked, if I were a dead house flipper.

I futzed in the house. My thoughts were whirling as I mindlessly stored supplies in the garage until mid-afternoon. Frustrated, and more than a little nervous about working alone, I called Myra.

"Hey, Myra. How about a glass of wine, or two, maybe three?" I asked.

"Oh, oh. What happened?"

"It's a long story," I sighed. "It ends with someone wants me dead."

"What? No! Do you want to meet at Ivan's?"

"Would you mind coming to my house? I'll pick up a bottle of chardonnay."

"Is five o'clock, okay? I'll get pizza. Hawaiian?" she asked.

"Perfect! You know me so well. Thanks, Myra, appreciate it."

I stuffed my cellphone into my bag, locked up, and ran to my Ford. The weather had turned overcast and rain splatted against the windshield as I buckled myself in. I locked the car as an extra precaution, knowing as I did, it was unlikely anyone would take me out in broad daylight. I sat back, the windshield wipers slapping back and forth, and collected my thoughts.

Out of the corner of my eye, I saw Randy's plumbing truck parked on the street in front of Fernando's residence. Don's admonition that organized crime was all around, in legitimate businesses and in the construction trades, registered. Construction? That would mean plumbing. Fernando had been a house painter in Arizona. Sarah's ex-husband had been a builder until he sold.

My mind raced, and I took a deep breath. *You're being paranoid again, Katelyn.* This is little Crocus Heights, Minnesota. Hardly big enough to support a mall, let alone organized crime. But what was Randy doing at Fernando's? I flipped my visor down and strained to see any movement in the vehicle or inside the house. Fernando's living room window coverings were closed. The van sat quiet. *They must be inside.*

I waited a few minutes until the neighbor who walked her dog every day, rain or shine, approached. Her hood was up on a yellow rain slicker and the little white dog sported a coat and galoshes as they passed my car. She looked at me as though she wondered what I was doing.

I nodded and drove off, with one eye on my rearview mirror, and headed home, making a quick detour to the liquor store, where I bought the economy-size bottle of wine.

Once home, I breezed in; Boots greeted me with a meow. I deposited my bag at the kitchen table and stashed the bottle in the fridge to cool. The cat was uncertain why I was home early, and nuzzled me, and I lifted him for a cuddle. Having none of that, he squawked, and I let him down.

Myra knocked promptly at five. I let her in, collected the pizza, and poured wine. I'd had a head start with a glass and was relaxed, talking myself down from the fish carcass.

"What happened?" she asked, taking the plate with food and a glass of wine.

"I was trimming trees in the back of the house, and found a dead fish wrapped in my sweatshirt on the front stoop. It freaked me out. Oh, dang!" I slapped my head. "I forgot to put the ladder away."

"The ladder will be okay." She shrugged. "But someone left a fish?" she asked, settling in the sofa. "Why?"

"Don't know." I grabbed my plate and sat across from her. "I called Don."

"And?" Her eyes lit up.

"He said it could be mob language. "Swimming with the fishes." As in someone wants me dead."

"Okay. Let's talk this through," she said. "The house is within walking distance to the river, right?"

"Yes."

"People fish on the banks of the river."

"Yes."

"Where was the shirt?"

"I took it off while working. It got hot. It wasn't raining, then. I left it on the front step." I frowned. "Where are you going with this? Some random person was fishing, stops and wraps a fish in my hoodie?"

"Well, maybe not just any person. It could be someone who knows you have a cat. It might be a gift for Boots?"

I looked at her like she'd lost her mind. "I don't think that makes any sense at all."

"Okay, but let's not jump to conclusions." She sniffed, peeved.

"All right. I'm a little touchy. I'm trying to figure this business out. Between the dead rats and now the fish. Something, somewhere is a little nutty," I reasoned. I didn't need to tick off Myra. There were too few people in my life right now.

"Yes. When you consider the rats, along with the fish, I agree. Something is afoot."

"So, what is it?"

"I think you're getting under someone's skin."

"I don't doubt that." I fingered my glass. "But these seem like serious threats." My nerves were frayed.

"Fernando?" she asked. "He's close by."

"He's been very nice to me. He seems very sad about Sarah's death."

"Or your plumber?" she asked. "He has access to sewer rats."

"I saw his truck outside of Fernando's when I left. I've been a good customer; I don't know why he'd want to threaten me. His dad was forced to sell to his partner in Mesa. He called the guy a crook."

"Huh. But, he's in Arizona?"

"Yes."

"Maybe they're just pranks?"

"Yeah. Maybe." I took another swallow of wine.

On the heels of Myra's departure, the phone rang. It was Wayne, and it was a relief to hear his voice.

"How are you and Gillie doing? Still loving Vegas?"

"It's great. But Gillie has this hankering to take a road trip. She complains about getting fat eating the danged buffets. She wants to see that rose garden in Mesa."

My ears perked up. "Mesa?" I had an idea.

"Yeah. They have over 10,000 rose bushes. You know how Gillie is with her flowers," he chuckled. "So, we're taking a road trip, see a few sites. It's at the Community College."

"I do. Gillie will love it." I'd given up on growing rosebushes in the northern region. "Would you do me a favor while you're visiting the city?"

"Name it, Kiddo."

"There's a plumber that works here. His father owned a construction company in Mesa. Just wondering if the firm is still in business. He said his dad went bankrupt during the housing crisis; a guy named Vincent Deala took it over. Fernando Garcia worked for the same company."

"Is Garcia the guy with the dead wife?"

"Yes."

"Small world, ain't it?"

"It sure is."

"Whatcha looking for?"

"Not sure. Anything that looks illegal." I chuckled, uneasy. I could Google. But if Wayne would be in the city, his up close and personal view would be more valuable.

"Whoa, you think Deala's involved in the gal's death?"

"I don't know," I hesitated.

Wayne heard the uncertainty in my voice. "Spit it out."

"It's almost too farfetched," I gulped. "I've had two rats left in the rehab, now someone put a dead fish in my sweatshirt. That gem was left on the stoop."

"Uh huh, 'swimming with the fishes,' *Godfather* movie," he said. "Forget which one." *Was I the only one who didn't know the connection?*

"I don't want to sound paranoid, but...."

"Sometimes, there's a good reason to be paranoid." He laughed. "There was always talk of funny business, corruption, when I was working. I never got close to it. But plenty of guys did. Somebody got a kickback for using a vendor, or paid somebody off to get a job. I'll be glad to check it out. It'll be a hoot while Gillie looks at every danged rose."

"Not a fan of roses?" I asked.

"Nah, it's not that. But they're a mite high maintenance in Minnesota. I just can't look at every bush, like she can. You gotta love that woman. She loves gardens."

"You're enjoying yourself?" I asked, sensing some friction.

"Having the time of my life, Kiddo. Could make it legal," he chortled.

"That's great." I was pleased. I wanted Wayne and Gillie to be happy when they got back to Minnesota. "Let me know how it goes touring the rose garden, and if you find Vinnie."

Chapter 22

The next morning, I headed back to Warbler. I'd calmed down and laughed out loud at the possibility someone had left the fish as a gift for Boots. Maybe they had and I shouldn't be so cynical. I parked at the rehab, grimacing at the ladder I'd left outside in my funk. I dragged the eight-foot wooden ladder inside to clean the light fixtures. I'd replace the outdated dining fixture. I had to shop it out, but wanted to wash the rest of them before the carpet installation.

I carted the heavy ladder to the bedrooms and the kitchen. *Note to self, buy a light-weight fiberglass model next.* The entry fixture would be the biggest challenge. If I couldn't reach it, I'd ask Eddy to clean it. The other lights I could reach by standing on the second rung. Finished with the upstairs, I tackled the entry ceiling light.

I positioned the ladder and eyed the span between the top of the ladder and the fixture. It would be a stretch and I wasn't a fan of heights. I set the spray bottle of ammonia and water on the attached table that holds the paint pan, and climbed the treads. When I reached the fourth step, I steadied my hand against the wall, took a breath and stepped on the top rung. It snapped.

In a surreal moment of slow motion, my arms flailed. Thrown off balance, my body plummeted, and my head slammed against the wall. The rest of my weight hit the basement steps. The last thing I heard was the bottle of cleaner hitting the floor, while the ladder toppled over as I slid.

"Katelyn? Miss Katelyn?" Fernando stood over me. His face was anxious as he peered at me. "Please. Wake up." He shook my shoulder, and I moaned.

"What happened?" My vision was blurry and every muscle and bone in my body ached.

"You had an accident. You fell. I heard you scream. I will call the ambulance."

"No. Let me rest." The last thing I needed was another big bill. I lay still for a moment, then gingerly moved my arms and legs. I felt the back of my head. "Ouch!"

"You must see a doctor. Please, Katelyn. I insist."

I sat up. "I got the wind knocked out of me. I'll be okay." I leaned against the wall and wiggled my fingers and toes. "See?"

"I do not like this answer. You could have a concussion?" He hovered, watching closely.

"Shouldn't you be at work?" I winced, looking up at him. Midday sunlight from the doorway flooded the entry.

"Yes. I came home for lunch. Do not worry. You are hurt."

"I must have been loud." I stretched and raised my arms and shifted my feet.

"It is no problem. I will take you to your doctor." His hands buried in his jean pockets, he leaned over, surveying my head.

"No. Fernando. Thank you. I will be okay." I moved the ladder from my legs.

"Katelyn! What's going on?" Don called from the doorway. He pushed past the ladder and entered the small vestibule. "What happened?" He crouched, brushing hair from my forehead, and scowled at Fernando.

Fernando's eyes widened, and he moved aside, tense. "She fell. I heard her scream."

Don looked at him quizzically. "How did you get in?"

"The door was open. The ladder blocked the entry, but I pushed it aside." He flinched under Don's questions, and said, "I will leave. You have help now, Katelyn," and he sidled out the entry.

"Door was open," Don repeated and looked after Fernando, releasing a sigh.

Not again. I groaned. "I guess I didn't lock up when I brought the ladder inside. Why are you here?" I winced and rubbed my temples.

"I thought I'd take a spin through the neighborhood on my way back to the station. Guess it was a good thing I did." He examined the ladder that lay next to my legs. "Rung is broken." With a scowl, he viewed the side of a tread dangling, attached by a few wood fibers. "Was this the step you were on?"

"Yes." I winced, my head beginning to throb.

"I'll take you to the doctor. Can you stand?"

"Yes. I'll call my clinic. I need my phone and purse, please." He retrieved the items and helped me up and out to his squad. "You should've called 9-1-1. You could have a concussion!"

"I can walk. My vision has cleared. I probably need an x-ray, which my clinic will do. I don't need a lecture."

"You can say thank you, anytime," he responded.

"Yes. I'm sorry," I gulped. "My head aches."

His forehead furrowed, he drove silently to my clinic.

"I'll get a cab home," I said, as he helped me out of the back seat.

"No need. I'll wait. My shift is over."

"You're sure?"

"Yes."

"Thank you, Don."

He smiled a full grin, and his gaze softened.

Feeling pampered, I met with my doctor; she took x-rays and checked every body part, recommending rest for two days to two weeks for a mild concussion. I protested that I had a house to finish, but it fell on deaf ears. As much as I hated to admit it, I felt as if I needed a good long rest.

I lay on the sofa with Boots for the next five days. Don, Eddy, and Myra took turns checking on me. Myra had driven Eddy to the Warbler renovation, where he locked up and drove my Ford back to the townhome.

By Sunday night, I felt back to my old self. It was Don's turn to check in, and I announced in his call, "I'm good now. Time to get back to work."

"There's something I need to tell you."

"Okay?"

He cleared his throat, "The top step on your ladder looked as though it had been cut. I didn't want to tell you at the time. You were hurt."

"Cut?"

"The underside looked as though it had been sheared with a hand saw. Not all the way, just enough to weaken the support, and so it wouldn't be seen by a casual observer."

"Good grief." I gasped.

"Fernando found you?" He asked.

"Yes." Silently, I thought through the day, and shook my head. "I doubt he'd have run over if he had anything to do with damaging the ladder."

"Maybe not. Just be careful." His calm, deep voice chilled me.

Chapter 23

I took Don's advice seriously and locked every door while I worked inside, or outside. I dumped the wood ladder and bought a lightweight aluminum model, which proved to be sturdy and easier to move.

It was early morning in mid-June when Dewey called about the carpet install. "I've got a rush job tomorrow," he explained. "It's a last-minute anniversary bash for a couple. We're on a small job this morning. I'd like to get in later today?"

"Yes. I can do that." I was eager to wrap up the inside while waiting on the siding.

We agreed on the installation for later in the day. Dewey's two-person crew arrived about twelve thirty that afternoon and worked until about seven o'clock in the evening, laying carpet on the upper and lower levels. In my opinion, new carpeting and paint make the rehab. I was feeling better about the house. There hadn't been any more threats with vermin or fish. Completion was within sight.

Although the installers had vacuumed, I went around the edges of the flooring, picking up threads of rug left behind.

I was downstairs, next to the washer and dryer, cleaning the edges, with country music playing. Alert to random noises, I heard a faint sound like a door slamming and turned the radio down, and listened intently. I stared at the doorway leading to the garage.

"Hey!" I yelled at the man striding into the room. I whipped off the vacuum attachment and waved it like a sword, advancing towards the intruder. "You need to get out of here!"

"Don't hit me!" He ducked, covering his head. "I know it's late. I forgot the carpet stretcher. Big job tomorrow and thought I'd take my chance that someone was here."

"Oh." I lowered the tool and studied the stranger. "It's you." He was one of the rug installers. "You could have knocked."

"I did. I rang the doorbell, too." He was a string bean, appeared to be forty-something, and spread his rough, weathered hands. "No answer."

"How did you get in?"

"Back door to the garage was open. The lights were on, so I walked in. Sorry; I'll only be a minute."

"Aargh. It's upstairs on the counter." I'd found the hand stretcher and left it in the kitchen. "I'll get it." I trotted upstairs and retrieved the tool. "It's kind of late to be at a job."

"Well, I don't have any reason to be at home," he said, annoyed.

I winced.

"Wife's dead. I live with my kid," he mumbled.

I examined him closely. He was about the same height as Randy of Randy's plumbing, with dark brown eyes, accented with dark shadows. He had salt and pepper hair poking beneath the edges of his ball cap. He lifted his hat, scratched the top of his head, and I glimpsed a bald spot.

"You're Randy Senior." I hadn't seen the resemblance earlier. A little bell went off in my mind. Why did Randy say his dad didn't live close? Was there another kid? Did Randy lie? If he lied, why?

"I am." He nodded.

"You were married to Sarah, the woman who was killed."

"Yes. And Sarah and I were still married!" He snorted. "You don't want to know what I think of that man she was with."

"Fernando?" I ventured, confused, "You were married to each other? You weren't divorced?" Fernando said living together had been commitment enough for them. A license was just a piece of paper. Apparently, so was a divorce decree.

"We would never divorce! Fernando was a passing fancy. I loved Sarah. I would wait. She knew that. But that man wouldn't let her go." His shoulders slumped, and he looked at the rug tool, then at the floor. "I apologize if I scared you. I'll go now."

"Yes. I'll check the doorbell to make sure it rings down here. I had the radio on, so I didn't hear your knock or the bell. So, you live with Randy, the plumber? He's your son?"

"Yep."

I digested that tidbit. "Your son has done work for me. He said you did handyman jobs?"

"I do. Flooring is my passion. I've known Dewey for years."

"My handyman is away for a few months. Can I call you if I get into a project I can't handle?"

"Sure." He stood straighter, brightened, and gave his rates. I walked him to the exit.

"This entry was open?" I asked.

"Uh huh. Not good for a woman to be working alone in an unsecured house, even if the neighborhood is safe."

"True." I was frustrated. "But you guys didn't come in this way?"

"We brought the carpet for the lower level in through the main garage doors, and then to the basement. No need to use this entrance."

"That's what I thought."

"We carried the carpet for the upper level through the front door."

"Yes." I nodded.

"Oh, wait." He slapped the side of his head, "Dewey came in through the back of the garage. He came around and propped the door because it would close and stop us from moving the carpet."

"So, Dewey must have forgotten to secure the back door. And I didn't check." *Drat!* "It wasn't his fault." I liked Dewey. Who couldn't like a guy who said floors were his life?

I locked up after Randy Senior, sighing. Mystery solved. Now I wanted to be sure I could hear the doorbell downstairs. There wasn't anyone to test the doorbell with, so I made a mental note of the ringer.

On the way home, my cell phone rang. I'm picky when it comes to driving and phones, so I pulled over and viewed the caller's number. It was Don. Maybe he had a lead on the vandalism in my bathroom, the rats, or the fish.

"Hello?"

"Katelyn. Have you eaten?" My spirits rose. Food and hunky Don Williams.

"I had a snack," I said, thinking of the trail mix I'd eaten while working.

"How about I pick you up and we get a proper dinner?"

"Okay. I'm driving right now."

"Driving and talking on the phone? That's breaking the law, unless you have hands free."

"I stopped by the side of the street. No lawbreaker here." I couldn't help the snark. My Ford hadn't caught up with Bluetooth technology.

"That's good." Although his voice sounded smooth, there was an undertone of worry.

"Is something wrong?"

"We'll talk later. What time is good for you?"

I glanced at the clock. "Give me an hour."

Chapter 24

Don was prompt. I met him at the door, taking a moment to admire his blond, silver-flecked hair. He wore blue jeans and a white shirt, open at the neck.

"Katelyn." He was formal and somewhat awkward. His expression somber.

"Who died?" My mouth engaged before my brain. I flinched and stood aside.

Entering, he tossed me a wry glance and shrugged.

"Sorry. Open mouth, insert foot," I quipped, uneasy.

"Ready?" he asked, pensively, his hands stuffed in his jean pockets.

"Yes. I'm starving!"

He finally broke into a smile. "Me too."

He led the way to his crazy fast Corvette and opened the passenger's side. I buckled up and held my breath as he started the car and revved the engine. Riding in the vehicle was always an exercise in white knuckle, back-seat driving. Shifting, he maneuvered to the freeway; the car gained speed. I closed my eyes and clung to the shoulder strap, sounds of the traffic echoed as we flew down the freeway.

Arriving at an all-night diner off the fast and furious 35W, I opened my eyes and exhaled.

Cheated death again.

He hopped out and came around, helping me out of the bucket seat.

"Nice ride, huh?"

I nodded. He smirked and took my elbow, propelling me to the restaurant.

After we placed our orders, he took a deep swallow

of coffee, sat up, and laced his fingers on the table in front of his mug. "I got the results of the DNA testing for Olivia."

"And?"

"She's not my child."

My gut thudded. "I'm sorry."

"Me, too." His eyes misted.

"Have you told her?"

"Yes." He took a gulp of coffee.

"That must have hurt." I grimaced at the thought she'd been rejected by a man she thought was her dad.

"She insists that her mother told her I was her biological father."

"Maybe, she did. Perhaps her mother believed you were?"

"I think she knew it wasn't true. Felicity may have lied because she didn't want Olivia to be alone in the world. Maybe her bio father had already rejected her?"

"And the man who adopted her died. Now, her mother's gone too."

"Uh huh."

"But you said there was a birth certificate?"

"Yes. There is." He gave me a brooding glance. "I pulled the document. There isn't any father listed on the certificate. Olivia lied."

"She'd seen the certificate. But her mother, Felicity, told her you were her father? And your DNA doesn't match hers. I hate it when that happens," I muttered.

He appeared bewildered.

"I mean I hate it when I'm right about stuff that hurts the people I care about," I submitted.

He reached across the table and clasped my hand. "Me, too."

Our food arrived, and our appetites were dull. We stared at the plates. He gave in and dug into a hot beef sandwich. I followed with my omelet. After a few bites, the food warmed our bodies, soothed our nerves, and we regained our composure.

"What now?" I asked.

"Don't know. Might do some more checking on Olivia, see if the rest of her story checks out."

"Sounds like a good idea. Maybe investigate death records. See if Felicity has really passed? What was her surname, anyway?" My mind was ticking away.

"Her maiden name was Hoffman. She kept it."

"So, Olivia's last name was Hoffman?"

"Actually, she went by Wilson. Her adoptive father's name was James Wilson."

"Okay. You do think Felicity is dead?" I prompted. "You don't think that's a story?"

"Yes, I think her mother has passed."

"Do you think her adoptive stepfather is alive?"

"Maybe."

"If you aren't her dad, who is, and where is he?"

"Don't know yet."

I pondered while I ate. "Olivia must have heard about you from Felicity. Why would Felicity have talked about you?" I shrugged.

"I thought about that. I told you we'd a brief fling, but she might have wanted more." His complexion deepened to a red, and he coughed nervously, fidgeting in the booth.

"Sheriff, I believe you're blushing. Are you embarrassed?"

"I was a different person then." He cleared his throat. "People change."

"Yes. They do." *Stop it, Katelyn Baxter. Stop falling for him.*

"So, how is the rehab going?" he said, deftly changing the topic.

"It's coming along nicely. They installed the carpet today. Oh, I found out that Randy, Sr., one of the carpet installers, is the father of the owner of Randy's Plumbing. Senior works for Fast Floors."

Don's expression glazed over. "How is this important?"

"Senior was wedded to Sarah Anderson in Mesa, Arizona, before she moved here with Fernando Garcia. But they never divorced."

"Yes." He paused. "She was living with Garcia, but married to Senior. We learned that when we questioned Garcia," he said, watching warily.

"Oh." He would know that. I blundered on. "It's a shame. Randy, Sr. seems like a nice guy. I wonder why she left him."

"Katelyn?"

"Yes?" I put my fork aside.

"You aren't getting involved in a murder investigation, are you?"

"No. I wouldn't do that." I batted my eyelashes.

"Don't be cute."

I sighed. "Any leads on the fish, rodents, or my broken mirror?"

"Vandalism and dead animals aren't priorities on the investigative list. Crimes against people, like murder, come before property crimes."

"Okay. So, is there any information on Sarah's murder?"

"You know I can't comment on an ongoing investigation."

I stared at him. "Dinner is on you, right?"

"Yes."

"I want dessert." If I couldn't get any information about Sarah's murder, at least I'd get a double-fudge chocolate cake covered with raspberry sauce and smothered with whipped cream.

He burst out laughing. "I can do that."

Later, Don left me at my door, with a light kiss on the forehead. I was wound up, high on sugar, and seeing him, and took to the internet to Google Olivia and her mother Felicity. More snooping I wouldn't tell him about. After a few minutes of searching, I felt a sugar letdown. Yawning I fell into bed, exhausted.

Chapter 25

It was noon the next day when I arrived at the rehab to find the siding contractor installing vinyl on the renovation.

Take your stuff and get off my property.

Burned out from the prior day of carpet installers, my night out with Don, and late-night Googling of Olivia and Felicity, I had overslept. I made it a lazy morning of paying bills and fortifying myself with strong coffee. I gritted my teeth and entered with mug in one hand and keys in the other. The carpet smell was overwhelming. I hurried around, opening windows to let in crisp air, while the sound of hammers echoed outside.

By the end of the day, they'd finished installing the material and removed the dumpster with the waste. After checking their work, I went back inside and breathed easy. It looked good. While I cheered the contractor's departure, there was a knock at the door. I peered out of the front window.

Fernando stood on the front stoop, clutching a container of flowers. I hadn't seen him since he'd found me after the ladder incident. I dismissed a moment of hesitation with another thought.

Perfect. I can check the doorbell.

"Hello, Katelyn. I hope you do not mind. The house is beautiful, yes?" Fernando said.

"Yes. It is looking good," I said. "It's been quite a ride. This was going to be an easy project." I snorted and did an eye-roll. "Thank you for coming to my aid when I fell, too."

"It was my pleasure." He beamed. "I am glad you

are well. Nothing good comes easy? I saw you had carpeting installed yesterday. I would love to see what you did?"

"Come in." He grinned and shoved a bouquet of daisies at me. "These are for you. They are a housewarming gift."

"Thank you. They're beautiful." It was a colorful assortment of gerbera daisies in a yellow vase. "I'll put these on the counter. It brightens up the space."

"You are welcome."

"I won't live here. I will list the house for sale once I add a little curb appeal." I had new house numbers, a mailbox, and flowerpots on my list for the exterior.

"I understand. It is a wonderful project. I will be sad when you sell. You have been a wonderful neighbor." He stood in the newly redone family room and viewed the space with a broad smile.

"Thank you. I have a small favor to ask?"

"Whatever you want." He spread his arms wide, grinning.

"I couldn't hear the doorbell downstairs yesterday. Would you mind pushing it while I'm in the basement?"

"Yes, I will be honored."

"Honored is a bit strong," I kidded.

He chuckled, and his soft brown eyes sparkled. "I am Latino. We are passionate." His dark hair shined. He was smooth-shaven, except for a shadow of a beard.

I smiled and went to the basement, and he headed outside, ready to test the chime.

"Go ahead, push the doorbell," I called.

Ding dong. I could hear it next to the washer/dryer area.

"I'd like to test the volume in another area!"

"Okay!"

I hustled to the 3/4 bathroom. "Try it now!"

Ding dong. I was satisfied the bell was loud enough. Last night, the radio and vacuum noise had drowned it out. I headed back upstairs.

"Thank you. Everything sounds good."

"It is my pleasure."

"Do you want to see the rest of the house?"

"Yes. Very much." His eyes lit up. I gave him the tour and was gratified by his exuberance as we walked from room to room. He stopped in the main bath and cocked his head. "This does not look like the mirror you purchased."

"It isn't. There was some vandalism. Add another seven years of bad luck," I said, with a grimace.

"I am sorry. It will be okay."

"I'm sure it's just a myth." *This place positively gets a serious sage burning.*

I walked him to the exit where he turned, and asked, "I also have a small favor."

"What is that?"

"I would like very much for you to be my guest for dinner."

"Oh." I was speechless. "Like a date?"

"Yes. A date. Unless you do not want to come? I do not wish to make you uncomfortable. You are seeing another man?" He shuffled his feet and looked away.

"No. Well, I'm not sure," I babbled. Don flashed across my mind. "I'm single." I shrugged. "Dinner would be nice."

A wide smile stretched across his face. "Perhaps this Saturday evening? I will cook my paella."

"All right." I gulped at the prospect that he would cook dinner at his house, but he appeared friendly and harmless with a bouquet.

"Six o'clock?" he asked.

"Sounds good." I gulped.

"Thank you. It is a date!" he said.

I watched his lightly muscled body as he practically skipped across the street to his truck. He backed out and waved. Watching from the doorway, I returned his salute. About to shut the door, Eddy drove up.

"Hey, babe. What's that all about?" He stepped down and motioned towards Fernando's departing truck.

"'Babe?'"

"What? You don't like 'Wifey.'" He threw up his hands, grinning impishly.

"Call me Kate, Katie, Katelyn."

"Katie it is." Coming from him, it had the same vibe, and was still annoying.

"What brings you here?"

"Just driving past, thought I'd see how the project was coming."

"It's nearly done." I stood aside and gestured him inside.

"Katie, this looks awesome!" He took the steps two-at-a-time to the upper level living area and twirled. His gaze narrowed when he spotted the bouquet.

"Flowers, too?"

"They're a gift from Fernando."

"Hmm." His gaze clouded. "Well, this place looks fantastic!"

"Thanks. It turned out better than I thought, given the storm damage and delays. Now it's going on the market."

"That's another reason I'm here."

"What do you mean?"

"I've been saving my overtime checks. I have the down payment for the Bluebird house. No more rent-to-own."

"That's great! So, you and Lola are . . .?"

"Nope. We're over. I know it's a big place for one person. But that could change?" He batted his lashes. I avoided the implication, and quickly flipped the light switch to view the bathroom, and asked, “Great bath, huh?” The fresh paint, new towels, and accessories staged the area nicely.

“Looks fantastic, Katie,” he whistled. “Too bad about the mirror.”

“Mirrors,” I corrected.

“Fourteen years, bad luck,” he chortled.

“Yes. I did the math.” I grimaced. “I’ve decided to have a major sage burning. Are you in?”

“Didn’t we already do that?”

“Double mirrors, double trouble, means twice the sage.”

“Sounds like a plan. Let me know when.” He winked. We toured the lower level, and I ushered him to the foyer.

“It’ll be soon,” I promised and looked across to Fernando’s deep sienna colored residence.

He observed my stare and asked, “So, what’s up with the neighbor? Did they ever find out who killed his wife?”

“I haven’t heard anything.” I hesitated and added, “He invited me to supper Saturday night. At his home.”

“Really?” His eyebrows rose, and he looked concerned. “And you said yes?”

“He wasn’t charged with anything. He seems very hospitable, gentle, even.”

“Uh huh!” He wrinkled his nose.

“It could have been an accident.”

“Blunt force injury?” he scoffed. “That’s no accident.”

“He doesn’t appear to be a killer. Besides, I’d like to check out his home,” I added, lamely.

“Now, that’s my Katie talking,” he said as he threw back his head and laughed.

“All right, already,” I protested.

"The snoop," he finished laughing, adding, "Be on high alert. What time do you dine?"

"Six o'clock."

"This Saturday?"

"Yes."

He threw out his arms and wrapped me in a bear hug. "You be careful!"

"Eddy!" His gesture caught me by surprise. "I'll be fine," I said, and I backed out of his grip.

"Stay safe!" He paused, gave me a somber stare, and left out the front entry.

"What in the world was that all about?" I muttered.

I had no sooner shut the door and went to the kitchen, when there was another rap. The knob twisted, and I stood at the top of the stairs speechless, as Don Williams entered. "Not locked, huh?"

"What are you doing here?" I demanded.

What is this, Grand Central Station?

He waited in the entry; his hat tucked under his arm. The sun cast a glow over his complexion, and his uniform was pressed and businesslike.

"Come in," I beckoned. "I've been giving tours; you may as well have one too."

"I'd like that." He trekked the stairs to the main level, gazing at the freshly painted and carpeted space. "Looks great." He saw the blooms. "Daisies. Nice touch."

"Yes. They're a gift."

"Uh huh." His voice was measured, and his expression veiled. He cleared his throat, "I'm sorry if I burdened you with my situation with Olivia."

"No problem. No apology needed."

"Anyway, I did some thinking, and I've decided that I'm going to cultivate a relationship with Olivia, even if she isn't my biological daughter. She needs someone in her corner."

"Even if she lied?" I asked, and winced.

"I believe she told the truth. I think her mother may have misled her. And that doesn't change the fact she's alone now. Without parents or family."

"So, you think you could be a father figure?"

"I think everyone needs someone to look out for them in this world. She was told I was her bio father. If I can be a reliable male figure for her, I will."

"She may still want to find her bio dad."

"And, she should. I will help her as best I can."

"That's awesome!"

"Can I see the downstairs?"

"Sure," I said, and I led the way.

When we reached the lower level, he made a beeline to the garage access door, trying it. "Good, it's locked." He unlocked it, and went through the garage to check the exit to the backyard, and tried that, too. "Great. Locked."

"Yeah. About the upstairs door, Eddy just left, and I plumb forgot to lock it."

"Uh huh. Eddy?"

"Yes. It's been busy today. First, Fernando brought flowers and invited me to dinner. Then Eddy came by to tell me he's ready to buy the Bluebird Street rental."

"Fernando asked you out? Like a date?" He stared; his cobalt blues darkened.

"Yes." I met his stare. "Is there a problem? I am single."

"Where?" He was terse.

"His home."

"When?"

"Saturday, six o'clock. Am I being interrogated?"

"He's still a suspect in his wife's death."

"He probably had nothing to do with it. He's always been a gentleman and appears to be distraught over Sarah's death."

"Katelyn Baxter. I can't tell you how to live your life."

I sensed a lecture coming and tried to head it off. "I'll be careful."

He stared. "You're trying to get close to Fernando to solve his wife's murder, aren't you?" He caught the flicker of guilt on my face. "Don't do it."

"It's just dinner. He's probably lonely. He was so happy to cook," I countered.

"Harrumph." He wandered through the garden level, his cool gaze taking in the window locks. My nerves danced, and my face reddened while he took his sweet time inspecting the rooms.

"I'll be going." He took a last look around the space. "It looks fine. Should sell."

"Thanks." His parting words felt weak, and I grumbled as I locked up after him. "Should sell," I mimicked. "How about saying, 'Fabulous flip? You've outdone yourself.'" I groused.

In the middle of my snit fit, Myra called.

"Are you busy?"

"It's fine."

"You sound cranky," she offered.

"Long story."

"I've got a few minutes," her voice thoughtful.

I relaxed and recited the events. "Fernando was here. He invited me to dinner, then Eddy came, and then Don showed up. It's been a full day, and it's not even two o'clock. Anyway, what's up?"

"Your day sounds more interesting. A date with Fernando?"

"Yes. Saturday night, six o'clock, his home."

"Are you sure that's a good idea?"

"You and everyone else thinks it kind of sucks."

There was a silence. "And, you don't?"

"Myra, if he killed Sarah, wouldn't they have

arrested him by now?"

"Investigations take time. There *are* other suspects—maybe Randy, or Randy, Sr.," she conceded.

"Yes. Well, maybe I could help?" I offered delicately.

"Oh my, in what way?" Her response was muted and held a note of fear.

"I don't know. Maybe someone with fresh eyes would see something the police missed?"

"That sounds like trouble, Katelyn Baxter."

"Great. That's the second time today I've been addressed by my full name."

"Excuse me?"

"Don lectured me. He said he couldn't tell me how to live my life." I groaned.

"I'm sure he meant well. How is he? He is such a nice man."

"He's fine. Yes, Myra, he is." I sighed. She made no secret that she considered the sheriff and I a good couple. "He said he's going to try to forge a relationship with Olivia. Their DNA doesn't match. He isn't her biological father."

"Oh. That's a shame. The news must have upset Olivia."

"Yes. But he still wants to be a father figure because her parents are gone."

"That's good."

"It is."

"You don't sound convinced."

"I haven't met her. It's hard to have an opinion of someone you haven't met."

"That's true. It seems her mother would have made some attempt to tell Don about Olivia."

"He says he didn't treat her well, and wouldn't take her calls."

"Oh. Not good, now he's trying to make amends.

Makes sense." She changed the subject. "So, Eddy stopped in?"

"He wants to buy the Bluebird Street house."

"Excellent! I'm thrilled for you."

"It'll be a relief to have one sold," I admitted.

"I'm proud of you!"

"Thanks. Hopefully, everything will go through." Eddy's track record with fiscal responsibility nagged at my conscience.

"It will and we'll celebrate!"

"Yes. Soon," I promised. I hung up with a thud in my stomach.

I hope you're right.

Chapter 26

Wayne called while I was getting ready for my evening with Fernando. I wouldn't call it a "date." It didn't feel right, and I didn't dress like I would with Don. I wore better jeans and a casual shirt, not so different from what I'd wear working at the rehab.

"Hey, Kiddo."

"Hello! How are you?" I was happy to hear his voice.

"Doing good," he cleared his throat. "I found your guy Vinnie."

"Okay."

"It's not a construction company. At least as far as I could tell."

"All right. What does it look like?"

"It's an appliance store."

I'd searched, but Google had come up empty for a builder. "Vinnie must have gone into appliances instead of home construction. He probably couldn't make it building houses."

"Yeah. But I don't think he's making money in stoves and refrigerators."

"Why do you say that?"

"I counted five appliances—stove, refrigerator, microwave, and washer and dryer through the front window."

"So, no inventory?" I scratched my head. "Was it open?"

"Nope. Sign on the door says to call Vinnie for an appointment. I got the number." I grabbed a pen and wrote it down.

"Thanks, Wayne."

"No problem."

"How was the rose garden?"

"Gillie had a ball! She found bushes to plant in Minnesota. She's gonna order when we get back."

"That's awesome! You're still coming in this weekend?"

"That's the plan."

I hung up, with toes and fingers crossed, that the plan stayed the same. And wondering why Vinnie had an appliance store with no stock? Buyers would want options.

I hesitantly approached Fernando's door shortly before six. I calmed my nerves with the mantra that it was just dinner and possibly I could do some digging. I could put to rest the idea that he had any hand in his wife's death.

I was about to ring the doorbell when the door flew open.

"Come in!" Fernando urged. "Come. I have vino for the paella. The food is nearly ready. We can visit while it is finishing."

I sniffed the aroma. "Smells yummy. Home cooking is a treat. Thank you for inviting me."

"It is my pleasure to cook." He beamed and ushered me to the kitchen. He wore a full white chef's apron over a short-sleeved, black shirt. The knit shirt displayed muscled biceps and a trim build. His dark hair was tousled, and soft brown eyes caressed me. I felt a chill in the air-conditioned house and shivered.

"It is too cool. I will adjust the thermostat. Please sit." He poured a glass of sangria. "I will be back."

I waited at the table and studied every nook and cranny in the neat kitchen. I couldn't resist a peek at the underside of the cabinet where I'd seen the spray of red, marinara sauce per Don Williams. It was clean now. I glanced out of the kitchen window and did a double take at the vehicle parked within sight of Fernando's house. A familiar black SUV. It flashed its lights at me. I blinked. Myra was behind the wheel. I squinted and made out the tall, lean form in the passenger's side: Eddy. I choked and gasped when a Corvette slowly rumbled past the SUV. Myra, Eddy, and Don were watching my date.

"It's a lovely night for paella and vino," Fernando announced, returning. "We will eat on the patio." I scooted back to my chair and took a sip of my wine, but gagged.

"Sorry, went down the wrong way," I gasped.

"The wine? It went down the wrong throat?" he asked. "Are you okay?"

"Yes." I coughed again. "Could I have some water and use the bathroom?" I gulped. He grabbed a bottle of water from the refrigerator.

"Thanks." I inhaled, wiping tears that trickled down my cheeks. I snatched up the water and headed to the bathroom. Secured in the room, I plucked my cell phone from my pocket and dialed Myra.

"What are you doing?" I whispered hoarsely. "Why is Don trolling the street?"

"We're on a stakeout. We want to be sure you're okay," Myra said, firmly. In the background, I heard Eddy's voice, "Hi, babe!"

"I'm okay. Fernando wants to eat outside. He'll see you!"

"We'll blend in. I promise."

"Don is driving his sports car. A RED Corvette!"

"Katelyn, do you feel okay?" Fernando called from the hall.

"Got to go," I said in a low voice, and disconnected. Giving a light cough, hoarsely. "Yes. I'll be right out." I opened the door and stared into Fernando's face. He gazed at me sadly, "You do not want to have dinner. You are calling a friend to—how you say—spring you?"

Busted.

"No."

He continued to study me, disappointed.

I thought quickly. "I phoned someone to check on Boots. He was sick and threw up earlier. Sorry. I should have said something."

"Your kitty? He is sick?"

"He'll be fine. But I asked someone to check on him."

"You are a good person. I will send paella home for Boots."

"He will love that." I had a twinge of guilt. "It smells wonderful."

"Let us eat." He beamed. "It is my mama's recipe." He rattled on while we walked to the kitchen and my mind raced. "I have a table ready outside. Please, let us fill our plates and we can enjoy this beautiful summer evening."

I helped myself to the dish. After he served himself, I followed to the patio. Spotting Myra's vehicle, I seated myself with Fernando's back to the SUV. A yellow cloth covered the small table that held a colorful vase filled with daisies, like the ones he'd given me.

Would a guy who likes daisies kill his wife?

I had another pang of guilt. "It's a beautiful night."

"Yes. We must enjoy it. The summers are so short."

A light warm breeze ruffled the branches on a nearby willow tree. In the distance, I heard the low hoot of a bird.

"Is that an owl?"

"Yes. The birds are nesting in the cottonwood tree at the edge of the woods." He nodded to the far end of the yard. Beyond the groomed lawn, there was a wooded area. “Dusk is their hunting time. Or early morning.”

“They are close.” I frowned, observing the tree. “Remember when the owl attacked Boots? Almost took him. I didn’t know their nest was nearby.”

“Yes. I was very sorry about your kitty. He has recovered?”

“Yes. Except for a stomach upset.” I smiled gamely.

“You take excellent care of your cat. That is important. How you care for your pet says much about you as a person.”

“Thank you.” I cleared my throat. “Was Sarah ever worried about the owls?” I remembered earlier warnings about the owls rushing people, intent on protecting their nests.

“My Sarah was fierce. She was not afraid of anything. You remind me of her.”

“Oh?” I gulped. Sarah was dead. Fierce hadn’t helped her. “Have they gotten any closer to solving her death?”

“No.” He sighed deeply, his expression troubled, “The police do not know. They continue to investigate and come up empty. They ask me so many questions. It wounds me. I would not kill my Sarah. It was an accident. There were marks where an owl attacked her, like your kitty. She ran to the house, slipped, fell, and hit her head.”

“Uh huh?”

“It is very sad.”

“So, you found her in the kitchen when you came home for lunch?” I squirmed.

“I found her blood on the edge of the kitchen counter. She must have had a dizzy spell and went to the bedroom. There was blood on the doorjamb. When she collapsed, she broke a bottle of her favorite wine which she kept by her bedside.”

“I’m sorry.” *He told the police she was in the*

kitchen. I was there.

"The police will not let me mourn my Sarah." Fernando's eyes filled with tears.

"That's tough." I maintained a mask of calm.

"But this is a celebration. Do not fret about that which we cannot fix." He held up his glass for a toast. "Here is to a beautiful and successful flip."

"Appreciate it." I smiled, and we clicked our stemware.

"You've had plumbing problems, no? The day you ran into my pickup, Randy's Plumbing truck was in the drive? I did not contact your insurance company. The dent is small, and the truck is old."

"I didn't report it either. Thank you." I forked a morsel of chicken. My thoughts raced. "Randy has done three jobs. He replaced the sink vanity top, installed flaps on the toilets to prevent rats coming through." I shuddered. "The last time, he did a plumbing inspection and fixed a leaky faucet."

"You know Randy is my Sarah's stepson? It is why she called him to do plumbing. She would say, 'keep your friends close, but your enemies closer.'" He chuckled.

"She considered him an enemy?"

"He was protecting his father. Senior was *loco*," and he drew imaginary circles around his head to indicate *crazy*. "He thought Sarah would go back to him. He was *muy loco*."

I recalled Senior from my encounter in the basement. He hadn't seemed crazy. Still, Sarah had been with Fernando for a year. It could be *loco* to carry a torch for a woman who was living with another man. Still, they hadn't divorced.

"Why didn't you and Sarah marry?"

"We were married in our hearts. That is more important than a piece of paper."

"Why didn't Sarah divorce Senior? It makes little sense to me to live with someone else when you're married to another," I said in a low voice.

"Ah. There is always the money problem."

"Money?"

"I am but a painter. She would inherit money if Randy, Sr. passed. He did not want a divorce. Sarah stayed married because she would lose out financially. He would not agree to the divorce because he still loved her and was sure she still loved him. He was *loco*."

"Hmm. But he installs carpeting? What money?"

"He made money when he sold the company. Randy, Sr. followed us to Minnesota after he sold. He wanted a simple life to lure my beautiful Sarah back. I told her to forget the money. We were happy together." He lifted his shoulders.

"Now Randy will inherit all of Randy Senior's estate?"

"Yes," he lifted his shoulders. "Even her life insurance. Senior is the beneficiary. He didn't agree to a change because they were still married."

"So, Randy, Sr. would gain financially from Sarah's death?" *And, with Sarah out of the picture, his son would get a bigger payday.* Randy and Randy, Sr. would have financial motives. Not to mention, it hurt Senior that Sarah was with Fernando.

"That is true." He ran a finger around the rim of his glass.

"Wouldn't that be disputed if she died from homicide? He wouldn't receive money if they convicted him of her murder."

"I believe that is true," he responded.

I wanted to ask if he and Sarah carried insurance on each other, but decided that would push the envelope. Besides, if he killed her, why would he tell me the truth?

It was dusk, with dim lighting from the patio lantern. Facing Fernando, over his shoulder, I saw the headlights of the SUV flicker on and off. My surveillance crew was getting tired. It made me feel all warm and fuzzy inside that the three of them were so worried about my welfare that they would go on a stake-out.

I finished my drink and rose. "Thank you. This was a wonderful dinner. I should go. Get an early start on the week."

"My pleasure." He reached for my hand, stroking it. "I hope we can do many more dinners like this. It is difficult to be alone."

My shoulders tensed, sensing pent-up passion under his declaration, and said lightly, "Yes. It can be lonely." Heading inside with my plate and glass, "I'll get my bag and call it a night."

"Don't clear the dishes, Katelyn," he protested. "I will do it."

"No problem. I'm going that way."

I stacked my plate and deposited the silverware in the sink. I hesitated when I saw the sharp knife Fernando undoubtedly used to cut the vegetables and chicken for the recipe.

Don't be silly, the cops would have checked the knife and block for blood traces. Besides, the insurance money would go to Randy, Sr.

I retrieved my bag from a chair, and he stood close, his body heat warming me. He reached over and wrapped his arms around my shoulders in a long hug, softly kissing my cheek. I froze, my thoughts scattered in different directions. He released me, and I croaked, "Thank you. I have to go."

Outside, I ran to my car parked in the rehab's driveway, ignoring Myra's vehicle, in case Fernando watched.

Two blocks further up, I pulled over, and the SUV stopped beside me. Eddy lowered the window. “Hey, babe.” Myra leaned over, a grin on her face, “Well?”

“Meet me at my townhouse,” I said. “I’ll fill you in. Where’s Don?” I glanced in my rearview mirror, and saw the flashy red Corvette rumbling down the street, closing the gap behind Myra’s car. He flipped on his lights.

“Never mind.” Trembling, I pulled into the street and drove home.

Chapter 27

Myra, Eddy, and Don gathered in the living room while I brought out wine.

"Hey, what happened?" Eddy asked. His face flushed with excitement. "Did you find something?"

"He didn't try anything, did he?" Myra asked, sniffing.

"Katelyn, you know I can't tell you how to run your life…." Don added.

"But Fernando hasn't been cleared of his wife's murder," I finished his sentence, adding, "He said Senior was the beneficiary of Sarah's life insurance."

"Yoo hoo! That could be Senior's motive," Eddy declared.

"That, and the fact they never divorced. It's a love triangle," I said. "But he says it was an accident. Why did Fernando change his story?" I pondered aloud.

"What do you mean?" Don asked. He frowned.

"When the investigators first came, he told the police he found her body in the kitchen. I heard him. He just now told me he found her blood in the kitchen, and her body was in the bedroom."

"Maybe he was in shock?" Myra submitted. "Could you have misheard?" She groaned.

"He *was* upset," I conceded, recalling the day.

"All the evidence is being investigated by authorities," Don said. "We knew Fernando and Sarah weren't married. That doesn't make him or Randy, Sr. a murderer."

"The house is ready to list. An unsolved homicide isn't a selling point. People want to know they live in a safe neighborhood!" I was peeved about the lack of updates on the case, and how tight-lipped Don had been about any progress.

"Chill, babe. All in good time," Eddy said.

"I don't believe many people would know about a death when they are house hunting," Mya said. "Besides, it didn't happen in *your renovation*."

"I suppose."

"It's not as if the killer is after random people. It looks like a domestic situation," she added.

"Yes, Katelyn. There have been no other murders in the area. We'll solve it," Don agreed.

That was small comfort with a house to sell, and a neighbor that appeared to be a kind man who wouldn't hurt a fly. I wanted it settled. If he was innocent, as he claimed, and questions about the neighborhood came up, I could say with conviction that he didn't kill his wife. I wanted to convince myself he didn't do it. I wanted to see Sarah's room. I had to get in when Fernando was away. Okay, maybe I was obsessed.

"Who wants more wine?" I held up the bottle.

Don looked at me quizzically. "You will wait for the police to solve this case?" he asked, his brow furrowed.

I poured the rest of the chardonnay. "Okay. I'll have to finish the bottle."

"Time to go," Myra announced. "I've got an early day. Home renovation doesn't stop on Sunday."

"Me too," Eddy chimed in, his eyes sparkling. "Myra's driving."

"How is the Hiptown project coming?" I asked, avoiding Don's glare.

"It's wrapping up. We'll have a tour soon," she promised. "It was nice seeing you, Don."

"And you, too. Be sure to say hello to your brother."

"Certainly."

Eddy leaned over and bussed me on the cheek and followed Myra out.

"Guess I should get going, too," Don said. He lingered in the foyer after they left. "Don't do anything foolish." He leaned over and planted a firm kiss on my mouth and slipped out.

Wow. I was in my happy place.

Sunday morning, I got ready to head over to the rehab with a mission firmly in mind. I would watch for Fernando and search his home while he was absent.

The phone rang. It was Wayne, and I was happy to hear his voice.

"Found your Vinnie Deala," Wayne said.

"Great!"

"You ever seen that DeVito character?"

"Danny DeVito?" I remembered the actor from sitcoms and movies.

"Yeah. He's like Danny DeVito on steroids. Short man, big voice. There's a poster of the guy in the front, on the phone. Fast talking, stocky guy. I called his number. His message says 'Call Vinnie for a good DEAL-a on your next refrigerator, stove, any major appliances!' He says, 'by appointment ONLY, leave a message.'"

"Really." The image of a fast-talking character selling appliances flashed.

"And he doesn't have any stock? Maybe there's a warehouse?"

"It looks like a big showroom."

"What do you think is going on?"

"He's not selling appliances."

"It's a front?"

"Yep. Like those stores selling exotic fish."

"Huh?"

"They have to travel to far off locations to get the fish, gives them cover to bring back contraband."

"You think Vinnie is dealing drugs?"

"He's doing something."

"Okay. Thanks, Wayne. I'll see if there's anything else on the web. Be careful. If this guy's doing anything illegal, he won't like you sniffing around."

"I will. You be careful, too."

"I miss you! When are you and Gillie coming in?"

"We're flying back this Saturday. Should get in 'bout noon," he said.

"That's wonderful!"

"Yep. Time for the fun to end. Getting hot here in Vegas. Seen enough casinos for a while," he guffawed. "What's happening there?"

"It's been interesting." I hesitated, not sure if I should tell him about my plan.

"Yeah? How's that? That death been solved yet?"

"No."

"How's the house coming?"

"It looks great." I added, "It would be better if they resolved the murder."

"Yeah. Makes for a cleaner sale. Safe neighborhood and all."

"Yes. It does."

"What 'ya doing today?"

"Oh. Catching up on a few odds and ends." He heard the evasiveness in my voice.

"Huh? You up to somethin'?"

"Wayne, you know me too well." I laughed, deciding to let him in on the plot. "I'm going to the renovation. I'll wait until Fernando leaves and sneak into his house to search Sarah's room. And they weren't married," I said in a rush, adding, "I'll fill you in when you're here."

There was a silence. Finally, he said, "Kiddo, you watch out."

"I will. I know he's gone every Sunday morning, like clockwork, so I'm heading over now."

"Ya sure it can't wait 'til I get back?"

"I want to sell the place as quickly as possible. I'd like the murder solved before it's listed. Well, you know. . .."

"I get it. Doesn't make me happy. I'd rather be there." He chuckled and added, "You be safe. We'll be back soon."

"Thank you. I'll be careful."

"I will." I hung up. Armed with the telephone number he'd supplied, I searched the web and quickly found Vinnie's Appliances. It was a bare bone listing with an address, but no website. Heck, I needed new appliances for the Warbler Street house, let's see what Vinnie says. I called the number.

"Vince Deala here, what can I get ya?" The brash, raspy voice answered. He sounded exactly like the picture Wayne had described. Short, stocky, balding and overbearing.

"I'm looking for appliances for a house I'm renovating."

"Yeah. Flipping houses is all the rage now!" He barked, ending with a harsh laugh. "What do ya want?"

"I need a stove and refrigerator, maybe a dishwasher." I hadn't tried the existing dishwasher, it looked in good condition.

"I got the best deala in town! Four hundred for stove and frig., fifty bucks for a dishwasher! 'Call Vinnie for the BEST deal,' That's my name, appliances are my game." He roared with laughter.

"For *new*?" I was all ears for a great deal on appliances.

"Yep. Brand new. Where do they go?"

"The rehab is at 123 Warbler Street, Crocus Heights."

"Let me jot down that address." I waited while Vinnie wrote.

"In Minnesota," I added.

"What the heck kind of crackpot are ya? I don't deliver to no fricking Minnesota!" and he slammed the receiver. I frowned at the phone. What, no Caller ID?

Dang, that was really a good deal.

I pulled into the drive of the rehab and parked in the garage, being sure to hit the remote and close the overhead door. Fernando's pickup was gone. The coast was clear. After months of working on the rehab, I'd gleaned the fact that he had a regular Sunday event; maybe he was even a churchgoer. Every week, without fail, his truck was gone. The other days were hit or miss as to when he was away. This was my chance.

My heart was thumping a million beats a minute while I strolled across the street. My plan was to ring the doorbell first, to avoid suspicion from neighbors. The morning was quiet, with most people tucked in, or away, much as Fernando. I tried the door. It was locked. I glanced around, checking for anyone who might be watching. No one.

I trekked to the side entry. Locked again. Defeated, I briefly considered what the penalty might be for breaking and entering. Shaking my head, I decided I didn't want to do time for any crime. Basically, I'm a wussy. There was one more possibility. I ambled to the back of the house.

The patio door was unlocked.

I slipped in. I didn't know if trespassing was a felony or misdemeanor, but hoped it was less than a B&E. Besides, I could say I forgot something if I was discovered. I'd just been there for dinner. Okay, sometimes I'm delusional; no one would believe that.

I crept through the residence; eyes and ears on alert for random movement or sounds. I passed the master bedroom and noted that he'd made his bed. A neat house is a happy home. I opened a door next to the living room. It was an office, which might hold some possibilities. Thinking quickly, I decided first I'd find and search Sarah's room, then return to investigate the office.

I twisted the doorknob to the room across from the master. Bingo. I paused in the doorway, scanned the space, and slipped in, closing the door behind me. The area held a small dresser, a side table, and a full-size bed. Although the furnishings were spare, the room was freshly painted and a new rug jazzed it up. I fought an impulse to rip up the floor covering to see if there was blood left from Sarah.

I kneeled next to the bed and scanned the carpet, telling myself even as I searched, it was silly. The rug was new.

Ribbit! Ribbit!

My new ring tone startled me. The croak of a toad humored me. Maybe someday, it would be Prince Charming disguised as a frog. Most likely, it would be a toad.

I scanned the text. It was Myra. *Where are you?* I muted the phone, slipping it in my pocket. "Not now," I muttered.

I studied the top of the bedside table. The contents were few, a lamp, a clock radio, and more dust. Opening the drawer, I scanned an assortment of notepads and pens along with a bottle of aspirin, allergy tablets, and breath mints. Pulling up on the sides of the drawer, past the gliders holding it in, I slipped out the container, placing it on the bed, and felt underneath. Nothing.

I reached to the underside of the bed table. My fingers moved under the table's top, and I gasped when I felt paper. I peered closely at the opening.

"OMG!" I stared at the find. I slipped my fingernail

between the envelope and the tape that fastened it and pulled it out. The packet was addressed "To be read in case of death." I tucked the envelope in the pocket of my jeans and scrambled to replace the drawer. I leaned against the bed, my heart pounding. My eyes settled on the bed stand and I moved the table away from the bed. Minute reddish droplets. My hands shook.

This isn't marinara sauce; maybe wine, or blood?

I took out my cell phone and snapped two photos, knowing my camera wouldn't do justice to the spatter. I repositioned the table and went to the dresser. One by one, I pulled out each of the four drawers and felt the underside. The drawers were empty. I ran my hands under the dresser top. There was nothing. He'd removed all the contents of the dresser. I opened the closet doors. They were empty, her clothing gone. I checked the time. The approximately ten minutes I'd been inside felt like an eternity, and I wanted to leave as fast as possible. Fernando's pattern had been to be away for several hours, but I couldn't be sure he wouldn't change, or that I hadn't been seen. A nosy neighbor could be watching or worse, have called 9-1-1.

I wanted to check out the office before I left. I quickly exited Sarah's space and doubled back to the first room. Hurrying in, I made a beeline to the desk. He wasn't as tidy in this space as the rest of his home. The surface of the desk was littered with bills, receipts, and paperwork. One item in the top bin of a document sorter caught my attention. I picked it up. It was a life insurance policy. Fernando had said Senior was the beneficiary to policies from Sarah, as his wife. But this document listed Fernando as the primary recipient. Did he lie about Senior being the beneficiary or did he forge the document? I snatched the paperwork, stashing it into my pockets.

I heard whistling from the hallway, and stopped. My

stomach plummeted, and my heart skipped a beat. Fernando was home.

I hurried to the door, held my breath, and listened to the muffled whistle. He was in the bathroom. The toilet flushed, and I heard running water. I darted from the area, tiptoeing through the kitchen to the patio exit. As I crept out, the bathroom door creaked.

Outside, I ducked around the residence. Once past the pickup, I straightened, trying to appear calm. Crossing the street, I entered the renovation via the back door of the garage.

Chapter 28

Once inside the Warbler house, I collapsed in a heap on the lower level carpet and gasped, curled in a fetal position, fighting to regain composure. When my breath evened out, I plucked out the letter, the policy, and my cell. I broke the envelope's seal and read the note.

To Whom it May Concern: If you are reading this, I am dead. Fernando Garcia has kept me captive and drugged. He is insanely jealous. I know now he baited the cougar in Mesa. Despite my efforts to convince him I wanted no part of a relationship or marriage with him, he persists. I am too sick and too weak to fight him. Please tell my stepson, Randy, that I regret the bitterness my relationship with Fernando has caused. I still love his father. I did not divorce Randy, Sr., and he remains my soul mate. I hope Vincent Deala rots in hell.

Huh? I pondered, Sarah and both Randys must have had a beef with Vinnie. Scanning the insurance papers, Fernando was the sole beneficiary of a cool half million-dollars at Sarah's death.

I called Myra.

She answered the first ring. "Where have you been? We've been worried sick!"

"What? Who's worried?"

"Wayne called. He said you were going to break into Fernando's house!"

Upstairs, there was the *thump, thump, thump* of a hard knock on the front door.

"Someone's here," I whispered. I decided to play possum. With my car out of sight, no one would know I was here.

"Who is it?"

"I'm not going to answer."

"Good idea," she advised. "Do you want to peek at who it is? I'll stay on the line."

"Okay." I ventured upstairs and checked the peephole. I saw the backs of a man and woman leaving. They were dressed in their best Sunday church clothes and I breathed a sigh of relief.

"They look like Jehovah Witnesses. I think they left a pamphlet. I'll get it."

"Okay. I'll hold," Myra said.

I waited until the couple was out of sight and opened the door a crack. Sure enough, they'd stuffed a flyer inviting me to learn about the faith between the screen and frame.

Fernando appeared as I closed the entry, my attention focused on the pamphlet. He shoved me aside and slammed the door, throwing the dead bolt.

"You have my property!" His eyes were black and his breath labored as he blocked the exit. "You have the policy!"

"I don't know what you're talking about!" I'm a lousy liar and he knew it.

"You LIE!" He charged me.

"Aaaaak!" I dropped the phone, praying Myra would call the police, and ran up the stairs. He followed. I turned and faced him, "Be reasonable. Why would I have any of your papers?"

He hesitated, as if he might buy it. Slowly, I backed into the kitchen. Blocking his view, I reached behind my back to a drawer where I stashed screwdrivers, a hammer, and a carpet knife. Next to me on the counter was the vase of daisies.

"You are correct." His respiration slowed, and his color faded from mottled purple to normal as he regained his composure. “I am sorry. I have been under a lot of pressure. Please forgive me.”

I relaxed. “All right. But you must go now. Out!” and pointed. He started for the door, then whirled towards me with his fists doubled.

“Aaaaawk!” I grunted and snatched the container of flowers, pitching the daisies and vase at his head. He ducked. The pot shattered against the wall. I yanked open the drawer with the tools and grabbed the closest one, a hammer, and held it up, threatening him.

“You killed Sarah!” I shouted, keeping him at bay.

“She wanted to crawl back to Senior! She could not do that to me. I would not let her! I took care of her!” His voice trembled, and he was close to tears.

“How did you do it?”

“She had boxes packed, ready to go back to that foul man!” He panted.

“Okay?” I looked at him blankly, the tool held high.

“She tried to leave. Her fancy wedding cake knife and fork were in one of the boxes.” He paused as though he was reliving the scene, his eyes glazed. “She even kept a reminder of their unholy union. I grabbed the fork and chased her in the house!”

“You took the serving set out of the boxes you tossed!”

“Yes. But she escaped!” His eyes grew large and his chest moved up and down with heavy breaths, and he glared. “I knew it! You were snooping!”

“How did you kill Sarah?” I demanded, yelling.

“I grabbed the bottle of sangria and hit her, and she dropped. The bottle slipped from my hands and spilled over the rug. It was perfect. She loved her sangria!”

He lunged and wrenched the hammer from my grip. I seized the carpet cutter, tripped the blade, and slashed at the hand that gripped the hammer. He howled and grabbed his fingers, a trickle of blood slid from under his grip. His eyes turned black with anger, and he dove at me with the hammer. I slashed again at his midsection and darted out of his path. Slowed momentarily, he clutched his gut and followed. I barricaded myself in the bath, frantically securing the lock.

"Go away! The police are coming!"

"First, I will kill you!" He shrieked and pounded at the door, busting the wood with blows from the hammer.

"Stop it!" I spit out a diversion. "You left the rodents! And the dead carp on my steps! You cut the rung on my ladder!"

The hammering stopped, and he gave a low, maniacal laugh that made the hair on the back of my neck stand up. "Such tiny little threats. You were supposed to leave! You DIDN'T go! You took my Sarah's boxes!"

Yikes. He knew I'd taken the cartons from the dumpster.

The strikes came faster and harder. *THUMP! THUMP!*

"But, why?" I demanded. Again, I tried to slow his progress.

"You were nosy. You were always watching me! I couldn't breathe!" Grunting, he pounded again.

That's true. Why did you lure the mountain lion to Sarah's yard in Arizona?"

"Ha!" He stopped, panting. "It was genius! She blamed Senior. She ran to me!"

"You tricked her!"

"He didn't love her like I did!"

THUMP!

The hammer made short shrift of the door. I looked around for anything besides my carpet blade to stop him. I grasped the plunger from beside the toilet in one hand, the rug knife in the other, and stood in the tub, waiting for his charge. He busted through, the force of his weight propelling him to the far side. I whacked him with the business end of the plunger and it threw him off balance. I jumped out of the tub, gripping both items as I ran.

As I dashed from the house, the noise of breaking glass and Fernando's curses echoed. I heard his heavy footfalls behind me. He dove for my legs and the carpet cutter slipped from my hand. While I struggled from his grasp, two police cars sped into the driveway, and four officers jumped out.

"He killed her!" I yelled, still gripping the plunger. Two officers grabbed Fernando, and I rolled out from under his hold. They cuffed him and stuffed him in the squad car. Don collected my makeshift weapon, and I scrambled to my feet.

"Easy, Katelyn," Don said.

My adrenaline surged, and I babbled, "He killed Sarah. He had life insurance on her. She was trying to go back to Senior, but he was drugging her! It's all in the letter."

"What letter?" He stared at me.

Oh, fiddlesticks!

"I found a letter from Sarah in Fernando's house." I might as well come clean. "Along with an insurance document."

"Breaking and entering is a serious charge."

"Patio door was open," I muttered.

His eyebrows rose; he said, "Theft is serious. Trespassing is a crime, a misdemeanor."

"I would have returned the items." I avoided his deep blues. "If the police didn't want them."

He relaxed. "Uh huh. You need to work on your poker face," he said with a grimace and an eye-roll. "You have the note and the policy?"

"Yes."

"I'll take them."

"Okay." I headed indoors, my shoulders sagged, and he followed. There were shards of glass along with remnants of flowers and the vase littering the stairs to the upper level. "Oh, for cripes' sake!"

"Looks like he broke a mirror."

"Dang it, anyway!" I marched to the bathroom, picking my way through the scattered pieces.

"That's another seven years' bad luck." He rubbed his chin. "I count three broken mirrors."

"Twenty-one years!" I groaned, surveying the mess. The remains of the wood door and jamb were in shattered chunks, the pieces of mirror scattered on the bathroom floor, the main level, and beyond."

"Sorry." Don's mouth twitched from holding back a laugh.

"Not funny!"

He sobered up, and said, "I need the evidence from Fernando's."

"I'll get it." I disappeared to the basement and retrieved the paperwork while he waited in the entry. "Here." I handed both over. "These should prove Fernando is responsible for Sarah's death."

"We'll need to authenticate the papers. Is there anything else?"

"Blood droplets."

"Not marinara sauce?" He gazed, his mouth set. "Investigators documented all blood evidence." He raised his brows.

"I took photos. They were in Sarah's room. See?" I found my phone and started searching for the images. "So, Myra called?"

"Yes. Pretty anxious, too."

"Yeah," I sighed. "He forced his way in."

"You should call her."

"I will." I found the pictures and showed the spatter images to Don. "Fernando said he chased Sarah inside with the fancy fork and knife from the boxes she packed."

"Yep." He viewed the photos. "We have these," he muttered under his breath.

Oh, oh. I bled on potential evidence and cleaned them, I thought, remembering the nicks I'd gotten from the serving pieces. My face flushed.

"Is there anything else?" Don asked.

"No. Not really." I bit my tongue.

"We'll do another search."

"Will you tell me if it's blood?"

"Katelyn, you know the answer to that." His sigh was heavy.

"Wouldn't this be part of the assault on me?"

"That's a fine line; if the neighbor assaults someone who trespasses and takes items from his home."

"Aaaaawk!"

"I have to take you in for questioning."

Resigned, I got in the back of the squad car, and Don Williams drove to the police station. Once there, he led me to his office. I sat across from him and stared, waiting for the lecture.

"Fernando and Senior both did business with Vincent Deala. Fernando painted the refurbished appliances and Vinnie bought Senior's business. He was Sarah's first husband, and a small-time drug dealer."

"OMG! Sarah's ex!" *Okay, they weren't new appliances.*

"Yes. She was beautiful, way out of Vinnie's league, and she feared him. It was a brief marriage and ended badly when Vinnie turned to dealing drugs."

"Figured it was drugs," I said.

"He used his appliance store as a front."

"Figured that too."

Don sighed and went on. "He would only sell an appliance if he was low on his supply of drugs. When he sold one, it came off the floor. He'd drive to Mexico and buy one or two at a time. He stashed the drugs in airtight containers and hid the drugs in the appliances."

"Don't they have drug-sniffing dogs at the border?"

"They do. He disguised the drugs and chose the busiest times to cross, when the border patrol was overwhelmed. He looked like an ordinary guy buying a cheap appliance in Mexico."

"Where is he now?"

"In a Mexican jail. He was caught at the border with drugs."

"I knew that deal was too good to be true," I muttered.

"What?" He glared at me.

"Never mind," I mumbled.

He relaxed, "Vinnie's drug money kept Senior in business, even during the peak of the housing industry. But Randy didn't know where the money came from. Deala was a silent partner and funneled money when Randy needed it."

"He didn't ask?"

"Why look a gift horse in the mouth? It got sticky when Vinnie discovered Sarah had married Randy Sr. He'd vowed that if he couldn't have Sarah, no one would. Then Sarah fled with Fernando, Randy Sr. followed, and then Vinnie showed up."

"Wow."

"Sarah was complicated. She married Randy Sr. when she worked at the company, but Randy Sr. was always busy. She was lonely. Fernando came along, and he can be very charming. She fell for him while Senior was trying to keep the business going."

Yeah, I get that. I understood lonely.

"But the economy was bad, and he sold," Don continued. "Vinnie paid him handsomely, because it was a money laundering game for him. Senior followed Sarah, and took odd jobs, like carpet laying, while his son got the plumbing company up and running. She didn't work because of her health problems that Fernando caused. Randy Jr. hated Sarah because she crushed his father's spirit."

"I don't remember seeing photos of Vinnie and Sarah in the boxes Fernando threw out."

"She hated him. She destroyed any reminders of their marriage."

"Okay." That made sense.

"Senior sold the business to pursue Sarah."

"Vinnie didn't catch on?"

"Senior followed Sarah and Fernando to Minnesota. Vinnie doesn't like the cold."

"So, he left them alone?" I asked.

"When the weather got warmer, he resumed his obsession for Sarah. She was a trophy, a beautiful woman. We think he was the prowler. Folks around here blamed it on kids. But Vinnie's short, he could be mistaken for a youngster. Sarah was wrong about the cougar in Mesa. Investigators suspected it was Vincent who baited the animal."

"OMG," I gasped. "How do you know?"

"The shoe prints left at the scene matched Deala's athletic shoes, size nine, according to investigators. He'd been harassing her in Mesa."

"The rats? Was that Vinnie?"

"No, Fernando left the box with the rat. Not hard to get a shoe box."

"But Vincent *was* in Minnesota?"

"Yes, then he high-tailed it back to Arizona."

"Uh huh. Who wanted me dead?" I felt my face

flush and I fidgeted. I sounded paranoid.

"It was always Fernando. He knew you were watching him." He stopped, and gave a weary glance. "Vinnie and Fernando knew each other through the business in Mesa. Fernando copied his methods of threatening people."

"So, Vinnie, Randy Sr., and Fernando all wanted Sarah, and didn't want any other man to have her?" I didn't envy Sarah's beauty and shuddered.

"Appears so. Vincent returned to his appliance store. Once Sarah was gone, his obsession ended."

"But didn't he know Fernando killed her?"

"If he knew, he didn't rat him out. He is a drug dealer, after all."

"Why didn't he go after Fernando?"

"He might have, except the last time he went to Mexico, he was caught at the border smuggling drugs."

Don waited, leaned towards me, his hands propped in a steeple. "Katelyn, I'll accept your account that the house was open. Maybe, you forgot something at his house the night before?"

"Yes. Yes, I did." I crossed my fingers behind my back.

"Uh huh."

Chapter 29

I went back to Warbler and took pictures of the mess left by Fernando busting into the bathroom at the Warbler renovation. I wouldn't be able to claim it on insurance. I'd already made one claim, and the damage, although annoying, didn't reach the deductible threshold. I ordered a door for the bathroom and bought another mirror.

Eddy helped me install the mirror and the new door.

"Getting to be an expert on mirrors, babe," he joked.

"Yeah, yeah." I was still smarting over the twenty-one years of bad luck. Once the mirror was up and the door in, I said, "How about we do a sage burning tonight? I'll check with Myra."

I called Myra while Eddy hung out.

"I'll bring the sage, wine, crystal stemware, and candles," Myra said.

"Wonderful!"

"And snacks."

"You're the best."

"Someone has to provide the proper ambiance."

"Thank you. I appreciate it. How about seven o'clock, after dinner?"

"I'll be there."

"It's all set for seven tonight," I told Eddy.

"Hey, that works. See you later, babe." He grinned and headed out.

I locked up behind him, dashed home, fed Boots, cleaned up, grabbed a sandwich for dinner and headed back to the house. I hoped the sage burning did the trick. This would cleanse the space and I could sell the newly renovated home without any bad juju attached. Now that the murder was solved, I could rest easy and assure any potential buyers that the neighborhood was safe.

On the way to the rehab, I saw Randy's Plumbing Co. was on a call. The truck was parked at the chatty neighbor's house. Randy was at the back of his van, loading his tools. On impulse, I drove past my rehab and parked behind him in the driveway where he was busy stashing his gear. I got out of the car and came up behind him.

"Hey, Randy!"

He jumped and faced me, slamming the truck doors.

"Sorry, didn't mean to startle you."

"I was finishing up." He glanced at the closed doors, took off his hat and rubbed his bald spot. He replaced the cap, tugging it down on his forehead. He towered above me.

"You heard that Fernando was busted for Sarah's murder?" I asked.

His face flushed, and his mouth twitched as he handled a wrench.

"Yep. Dad's happy they got him." He eased toward the driver's seat.

"I'll bet. Your dad seems like a nice guy."

"He is."

I looked around him at the van. A movement had caught my attention. An item dangled, caught in the bottom of the double van doors. I stared, trying to make out the object.

The confrontation with Fernando flashed across my mind. He hadn't copped to the rats. He'd said they were meant to scare me. I gaped. "That's a tail! The tail of a brown Norwegian rat!"

"What?" Randy moved to block my view. "Mind your own business, lady." His voice was cool, menacing, as he gripped a plumber's wrench. "Get out of my way! Move!"

"You put rats in houses for. . . what? To make like a wannabe mobster, like Vinnie Deala? To threaten people? For more business?" I yelled. "You're a bully and a thief!"

"You're crazy, I don't have to take this." He jumped into the driver's seat.

"What about the exterminator? Tim?" I ranted. "Is he your business partner, too?"

"I work alone, lady," he sneered.

"What about Fernando? He learned from Vinnie, too!"

"That's different." His voice was low and hard. "Move your rust bucket, or I'll do it for you!"

"Don't you dare! And my car is not a junker! What are you hiding in there?" I gasped and went for the back doors, throwing them open.

Inside was an overturned bucket spilling dead rats. I screamed again. My shrieks brought him out of the front seat, and he came at me with the wrench, "Shut up, you bitch!"

I dodged him, screaming louder. "Help!"

He slammed the doors, brandished the wrench, ran to the driver's side, and hopped in behind the wheel. On the way, he hurled the wrench at the windshield of the Festiva, hitting a sweet spot, and breaking it.

He started the truck and, revving the engine, backed into the front of the Ford, crunching the fender. The hood buckled. He threw the truck into drive, and jerked the wheel to the right, making a large U-turn into the neighbor's yard, leaving ruts, and the car in a heap. He squealed his tires and sped away.

I dashed to the car and cranked the engine. It sputtered, hissed, and died. I got out, stepping through a stream of water and antifreeze spewing from the radiator onto the drive. Resigned, I called 9-1-1.

Myra came promptly at seven, Eddy was a few minutes late.

"You wouldn't believe the day I've had," I grumbled. I took the basket of sage, snacks, candles, wine, and serve ware from Myra, placing it on the counter.

"What?" Myra asked. We stood in the living room of the Warbler rehab.

"Randy, Jr. left the rat in the toilet, Fernando left one in the shoebox and the dead carp." I was grim as I unloaded the carrier. "They learned how to threaten people from Vinnie, the wannabe mob boss."

"Say what, babe?" Eddy was astonished. I laid out the spread of goodies.

"Randy Jr. was in cahoots with Fernando. He suspected Fernando killed Sarah."

"Why didn't he call the police?" Myra uncorked a bottle of white wine.

"He had no love for Sarah. He didn't like his father getting back with her. If push came to shove, and they charged his dad with Sarah's murder, he'd have ratted out Fernando. As it was, he was glad Sarah was out of the way, and the rats were a bonus for his startup business. 'Keep your friends close, and your enemies closer.'"

"Oh, my," Myra gasped. "How do you know all of this?" She poured chardonnay into a crystal glass.

"Randy had a bunch of rats stored in the back of his van. When I found them, he rammed my car. It's toast. I had it towed to the junkyard."

"Oh no! Katelyn!" She inhaled.

"Yep. The cops caught up with him and busted him for leaving the scene of an accident. He's in jail. They're investigating him, and his business practices."

"OMG. Here." Myra offered me a glass of wine.

I took a gulp.

"Don't worry about your car. My old SUV is still good to go. It's only taking up space in the garage." She had lent me the cushy SUV after my car's engine blew in a chase with the bad guys during my first renovation.

"Thanks, Myra."

"Sorry, babe." Eddy threw his arm around my shoulder and hugged me. "Rough day."

"Yep." I nodded.

"Shall we proceed?" Myra asked and twirled in the room. "This looks great! You won't have any trouble selling this place."

"Yeah. Nice job," Eddy chimed. "Especially with that boss mirror and new bathroom door."

We each lit a bundle of sage and placed it on a plate. I lit the lavender-scented candles and recited my intention for a clean home and quick sale. We walked through the dwelling, moving the herb into all the nooks and crannies. We finished blowing out the candles and crossed ourselves.

"It feels better," Myra said.

"It does, doesn't it?" I agreed. I forgot about the miserable day and viewed the house. Neutral colors and carpet updated the split-entry, and it appeared spacious and inviting. "I can hardly wait for Wayne to get home. I want to show him how it came out."

"When will he and Gillie be back?" Eddy asked.

"This Saturday."

"Well." Myra smiled her Mona Lisa smile. "We must do something special."

"Hey, let's toast to a fresh start," Eddy urged.

"Eddy is buying the Bluebird Street house. Wayne and Gillie are officially a couple," I announced.

"My Hiptown construction is nearly finished," Myra added.

With that, we freshened our glasses and held them up to one another, clicking the crystal, chanting in unison. "To new beginnings!"

Chapter 30

Myra and I met at the new Hiptown house.

"This is wonderful!" I was awestruck. The exterior was a beautiful shade of gray, which blended with the existing neighborhood housing. The porch had been replicated with half walls mimicking the original dwelling. New outdoor chairs and plants welcomed visitors on the porch.

"Yes. After the last visit from Bernie, the spirits were finally gone, the workers returned, and the job went off without a hitch."

"Wish I could say the same."

"You had special circumstances." She gave me a wry look.

"You had rogue spirits," I protested.

"Yes. We each had issues." She sighed. "But it looks fabulous." The exterior of the home had the lines of the Craftsman style home that had formerly been there, but better. It invited new residents with a bright, shiny-new presence.

"Myra, do you think it could have been vandals, and not a spirit, that spooked the workers? Maybe, even Deala? He'd been in Minnesota, maybe he saw you, and wanted to make mischief?" I shrugged. "I'm probably paranoid."

She crossed her arms, tilted her head, and studied the outside of the house. "I suppose he may have had a hand in it. But we won't really ever know."

"Not as long as he stays put in a Mexican jail," I said.

"Let's hope he does. For my money, Bernie did the job," and she chuckled. "Let's go inside." Indoors, the home was as beautiful as the outside. The open floor concept made the dwelling spacious and welcoming. Design elements of the era had been incorporated with moldings and doors. We took a tour of the upstairs bedrooms.

"No window seat?" I asked, surveying the room.

"Some things are better left out." She gave a wistful smile mingled with regret.

"True enough."

While I oohed and awed over the home, she asked, "What time are Wayne and Gillie expected back?"

"Saturday morning. Can't wait," I said. "It's been a long stretch. The townhouses have been so quiet without neighbors. Not to mention, rehabbing the Warbler house without Wayne has been a nightmare."

"Yes. That was quite the project." She nodded.

"Amen. From creampuff to nightmare." I grimaced.

"But it's done and looks great," she reminded me.

"It is. Thank you."

"I have a few ideas to welcome the newlyweds home." Her hazel eyes held a mischievous twinkle.

"What do you have in mind?"

"Well. . .."

I giggled while Myra filled me in on her plans for a welcome home party and reception.

I had access to Wayne's unit and borrowed the key to their new unit, purchased by the couple as their "together" home. Crossing my fingers, I explained to Wayne that I wanted to be sure everything was good for their arrival. They'd turned the water off in their absence and the unit needed cleaning.

"Sure. Ya go ahead," he said. "We're pumped to be coming home."

"I'm super happy to see both of you!"

Myra and I decorated the home, set up a table, brought in potted plants, and rented an arbor. We arranged chairs in front of the arbor for guests to watch the wedding ceremony.

While adorning the arch with artificial roses and greenery, I said, “Myra, I don’t know how Wayne and Gillie feel about an official wedding. Wayne said they were taking their vows without making it a legal marriage. He called it the ‘commitment’ ceremony package.”

“This is a welcome home and combination reception party. It’ll be up to Wayne and Gillie if they want to make their commitment legal, or if they want to repeat their Las Vegas vows. I’m only giving them options.” She smiled impishly.

“Sure.” What Myra wants; Myra gets.

“You invited Don?”

“Yes, and his adopted daughter.” I grinned.

“He’s such a nice man.” Her eyes sparkled.

“Yes, he is.” I did an eye-roll. “I invited Eddy, too. And Broccoli Bob.” I coined Bob “Broccoli Bob” from an incident with rotting broccoli. He and Gillie had designed and maintained the memorial garden for Ariel, at her parent’s request.

“The more the merrier. I invited my brother, the police chief.” Myra said, and sniffed.

“Of course.”

It was agonizing not to tell Wayne and Gillie what we’d planned. I picked them up at the airport and drove them home. When they opened the door to their new unit and saw the decorations, Gillie’s face lit up. “Oh, Wayne. This is wonderful. We’d better get dressed.”

“Yep. Sure ‘nuff should.” Wayne threw his head back and guffawed. “Kiddo, you didn’t have to do all this.”

"It was Myra's idea, and we wanted to. Welcome home!"

The patio of Ariel's refurbished unit was lined with urns filled with flowers. At the far end was a white arbor. Just beyond the rose-decorated arbor was the garden Broccoli Bob had carefully cultivated during the months that Gillie and Wayne were away. It was in full bloom, with zinnias, dahlias, and other summer flowers between the tomato, squash, and pepper plants.

Bernie, the ghostbuster Myra had hired for the Hiptown house to clear the lot of paranormal presence, stood at attention under the arbor. He smiled reassuringly; his dark thin strands of hair askew. He wore a double-breasted white suit and rose-colored sunglasses.

The sound of Elvis Presley crooning *Love Me Tender* came from a boombox at one side of the arbor. The couple stopped, momentarily speechless.

"Oh, Wayne," Gillie murmured, "this is wonderful!"

"Yep." He gulped. "It sure is somethin'." He wore a white dress shirt, dark vest and matching slacks. His long, gray hair was braided. Adjusting his tie, he grinned. "Gillie? Ya want to make this legit?"

"I'd love to, Wayne." She looked at him, adoringly. She wore a lacey, tea length, apricot-colored dress. Her pixie hairstyle had the same hue, along with a streak of deep rose. A daring look for the woman known for matching sweatpants and hoodie outfits. She held a bouquet of red, long-stemmed roses.

"Me too! Let's git 'er done!" He grabbed her hand, and she left the bouquet with Don's daughter. They strolled along the path to the sounds of Elvis crooning, and stopped in front of the arbor where the ghostbuster, Lyft driver, and marriage performer waited.

Bernie spoke solemnly, "By the powers vested in me

. . .”

I stood between Eddy and Don. Myra and I dabbed at our eyes, while Eddy shuffled his feet, coughed, and sniffled. Don stood tall and attentive while he watched the ceremony, a broad smile stretched across his face, his adoptive daughter by his side.

There wasn’t a dry eye in the room as Wayne and Gillie recited their vows. Don reached for my hand and squeezed it. Our eyes locked. Eddy took my other hand and held Myra’s.

As we gazed at one another, a feeling of peace settled in, and the long, lonely journey faded. Then Don leaned towards me, his soft lips brushing against mine. In a low deep voice, he said, “Katelyn, let’s get married.”

“OMG!” I gasped.

The End

Katelyn's Home Improvement Tips

1. To remove rust stains from a porcelain sink, make a paste of lemon juice and table salt. Rub the mixture into stain and let sit. If stain is stubborn, apply again.

2. Rats entering through a toilet is the stuff of nightmares. Putting bleach in the toilet will suffocate a rat within fifteen minutes. A plumber can install a flap to prevent creepy creatures from swimming into the fixture through the sewer line.

3. Soak grimy barbecue grates overnight in a plastic garbage bag with ammonia. Wipe clean the next day.

4. Check other homes on the market in your area to see what your competition is when planning home improvements if you plan to sell.

5. Watch DIY shows to get ideas for updating your home.

6. Deep clean the bathroom with a solution of half vinegar and half dishwashing soap. Heat the vinegar and add the soap. Put in spray bottle. Don't shake, mix gently.

7. When removing wallpaper, use a solution of 50/50 hot water and white vinegar. Score paper, spray solution, wait fifteen minutes, then remove with a blade. Repeat as needed.

8. Or, use equal parts fabric softener and water in a spray bottle to remove wallpaper. Score paper, and let solution soak in 15 minutes before removing.

9. Clean a stainless-steel sink by rinsing first, coat with baking soda, scrub in direction of stainless grain, spray on vinegar, rinse, and buff with olive oil.

10. Sometimes buying products can be a better investment than DIY, i.e., framing out a mirror vs. purchasing.

11. Use washing vinegar (available at the dollar store) for dark clothes instead of laundry soap to keep dark clothes looking their best.

12. Clean fixtures with the bulbs off, and wash windows on cloudy days. Streaks will show up under low light.

ACKNOWLEDGEMENTS

Many people deserve my gratitude for their support, friendship, and work associated with the Home Renovator Series, including libraries and bookstores. My sincere thank you to the following:

Thank you to Betty Borns, for our many years of friendship, fun and more: Joe Sebesta and Judith Anne Horner, beta readers; Julie Seedorf, and Twin Cities Sisters in Crime; Guppies; the Word Whippers Critique Group: William Anderson, Cathlene Buchholtz, Dale Butler, Barb Danson, and Mary Rodgers for their continuing support.

About the Author

LETHAL FLIP is the third home renovator cozy mystery novel by M. E. Bakos. The first was **FATAL FLIP**, followed by **DEADLY FLIP**. Her short story, “Champagne Wishes and Caviar Dreams,” was published in the Cooked to Death Anthology, Vol. V, 2020, featuring characters from the series.

Mary is an enthusiastic fan of home improvement shows and has done numerous home projects through the years.

She is a member of Twin Cities Sisters in Crime, the SINC Guppies Group, and an alumna of the University of Minnesota. Her mystery short stories have also appeared in Twin Cities Sisters in Crime anthologies. She resides with her husband, Joe Sebesta, and their spoiled Morkie, (Maltese/Yorkie) Chipper, in Minnesota.

She welcomes reviews and comments from readers.
Please email her at: mebakos@yahoo.com
https://www.facebook.com/mebakos/
https://mebakos.wixsite.com/author

Thank you for reading Lethal Flip.

If you enjoyed this book, please consider posting a review on your favorite retailer's website.

FATAL FLIP, DEADLY FLIP, and **LETHAL FLIP** received five-star reviews from Reader's Favorite.

www.ingramcontent.com/pod-product-compliance
Ingram Content Group UK Ltd.
Pitfield, Milton Keynes, MK11 3LW, UK
UKHW041856190726
13854UKWH00002B/934

9 798985 077087